the
DILEMMA

ROWLAND STEWART

the
DILEMMA

ROWLAND STEWART

foxboro press

Address inquiries to: editor@foxboropress.com

Local New York: (212) 537-9430
Toll-Free: (800) 980-1390
Fax: (800) 980-1390

ISBN 13
978-0-979335b-9-3 (hard cover)
978-0-979335b-8-b (soft cover)

Library of Congress Control Number (LCCN)
2007907196

Manufactured in the United States

First Edition

For Casey
For keeping an open ear

Ignorance is bliss
—Anonymous

- one -

At the fork in the road, Aziz turned left. He followed the dust-covered road for another twelve kilometers, alongside the small tributary that fed into the Tigris River. The green bank extended upward where the brown desert took hold, squeezing life from the vegetation. His progress remained steady. Not much time.

Less than an hour ago, the phone call awakened him from the first good sleep in four nights. He was told by the others only what they thought he needed to know—the lab had to be moved. They were fairly certain that the Americans knew its location. They could not be sure, but they wouldn't take chances on destroying so many years of work because of simple carelessness.

He wrapped his left hand around his long beard, pulling it downward to a point near the middle of his chest. He repeated the maneuver several times, as he focused his thoughts.

Packing thirteen years of work in four days was not an easy task—only the essentials could go. Some of the larger equipment, such as the centrifuge, was specially modified and much more difficult to move. The later work was less theory and much more engineering. Purification, high volume production, and aerosolization all required different equipment than what he had trained with throughout his postgraduate studies in California.

A terrible thing, he thought. *Friends were now enemies, enemies were friends.*

He looked out the cracked windshield as he bounced on the small, elevated dirt road beside the riverbank. He had run along a similar riverbank as a child, dreaming of becoming a world famous scientist, making some kind of revolutionary discovery that would change the world forever. He had rummaged through the mud along the banks of the tributary, his earliest biological laboratory. He had started with large bugs: insects like crickets and water spiders. After his mother bought him his first child's microscope from a bazaar in Tikrit, he peered through the small lens into the vast expanse of the microscopic world and was hooked.

The years he had spent in Berkeley spoiled him to more temperate climates. Now, after eight years back home, he was miserable. The desert heat blew through the open windows like a blast furnace. Beads of sweat crawled down his face. He raised his left wrist and wiped the moisture away from his eyes. Dust clung to the windshield partially obscuring his view of the road, but he could see the small village ahead, his home for the last six months.

The lab was moved here, to be out of sight. The villagers were not happy with the Americans, so nobody spoke of the lab. They knew this work could free them of their occupiers.

He turned the small, rusted yellow car from the river levee down towards the village, just a few hundred yards ahead. He saw several small boys kicking a soccer ball outside the low mud wall that surrounded the village.

A fierce white light nearly blinded Aziz just before the shock wave tossed his car from the levee ramp where it tumbled over and over down the embankment, coming to rest upside-down in the field. Thick dust filled the air, almost choking him. Aziz came to rest on his right side with his back against the rear quarter of the car. He eased himself out through the shattered rear window and lay down, face to the sky. Blood oozed down from a large gash in his forehead across his nose and dripped further down his ear and onto the dirt.

He sat up slowly and looked back to the village where the bomb had hit, just thirty seconds earlier. The boys who were playing soccer were gone. Aziz saw no signs of life until a screaming woman in a blood-soaked burqa came running out of the village.

Aziz stood up and ran forward into the village. His head pounded with each frantic step.

They hit the mosque, he thought.

Very little of the building remained. A ten-meter crater with very little debris had taken its place.

He immediately refocused and ran further down the street towards the small metal building with the white van sitting outside, still upright. The engine was running.

Amazing.

Aziz and his staff were all shaken, but alive. However, he knew that the reprieve was only temporary. The Americans would be back, and they would not miss a second time.

The technicians inside the building weren't hurt, except for some small wounds from the flying glass. The building remained standing—shielded by several small mud structures between them and the mosque.

"No, no! There's no time for the computer. Just grab the data disks," screamed Aziz in Arabic. "What about the culture sets and the broths in the incubator?"

"Batches one... batches one through twenty-three were sent out yesterday. We still have twenty-four through eighty left to go."

"And what about strain B103FT?"

"Most went out yesterday, sir."

The three technicians and Dr. Aziz hurried to pack the remaining essentials of their work into the van waiting outside. Six years of brilliant work was now reduced to some computer disks and a few bacterial cultures.

"They're crazy," said the technician. "If this place explodes, this stuff will go everywhere."

"They know exactly what they're going after," said Aziz.

He knew about the advanced weapons of the United States. The electrical smell was unmistakable, a plasma bomb, which would effectively sterilize ground zero.

Aziz heard jet afterburners in the distance.

There was no time for pain. Suction caused the building to implode on one side and the flash vaporized most of it, including everyone inside. The second explosion rocked the area for a mile around but didn't completely destroy the van that they had been loading, which broke apart and spilled its contents into the prevailing westerly wind.

♦ ♦ ♦

The sand was a problem to Lieutenant Gray—a big problem. Different from the sand on the beaches of his native Texas, this sand was more like powder, lodging in every orifice and in all of his equipment. He could barely run in it, particularly with forty-five pounds of battle gear. The stop to rest was necessary, but he knew it would be short.

The Marine team advanced rapidly from the south. The objective was to secure the small village ahead of them, known to shelter at least six men wanted by the United States. The earlier briefing included details of the targets, but little about what they were doing. The orders were simple—capture or kill these men and any other threats found in the village.

To the west, the sunset fused the orange sky with the dull yellow of the desert. The light was low but it was enough.

The village ahead appeared small, perhaps a hundred huts in varying forms.

Gray crouched behind a mud-brick wall. At about three feet high, the wall served as excellent cover. The other men approached silently and secured positions along the wall. Gray raised his hand and signaled with a fist to hold here. He looked forward to assess.

About forty yards to Gray's left, Porter put two fingers towards his own eyes and pointed to his partners. He then held out his hand, palm-down, fingers together. He pointed to the two Marines next to Gray.

Gray nodded.

Porter and the other two men crawled over the low wall and approached the first hut in the village. The other nine team members remained at the wall.

The men at the wall drank some needed water before moving ahead. He knew that water was the most precious resource; the packs on their backs added weight, but the ability to drink while moving was invaluable.

The radio silence broke.

"Porter to Gray." The radio crackled in Gray's ear.

"Over."

"No activity in west end. Forward approach covered."

They spread out in three groups. In each, two men ran forward about thirty yards while the other crouched, aiming his MP-5 compact submachine gun forward in anticipation of enemy fire. They alternated, advancing slowly.

Gray had experienced close contact hostile fire more than anyone in the team had, serving four years in Iraq across two wars. He knew enough to temper youthful enthusiasm with a veteran's paranoia. The village appeared harmless as they approached, but he knew that the unknown could hide great harm. The three groups of men advanced on the first house on the outskirts of the village. It was a small structure; the exterior was dried mud, and a rusted corrugated tin roof covered the top. Shadows covered the village.

"Stop shy a hundred yards. Two groups forward to back wall. B group, C group…forward."

Gray spoke into the radio connected to his helmet, which linked him to the eleven men in his command.

The men moved ahead in silence until they reached the back wall of the house.

"C group go left. B group go right."

The men divided, surrounding the building from opposite sides.

"All clear front. We're going inside."

Static crackled on the radio, distorting the voices.

"Enter with caution, standard cover from back," said Gray.

After an uncomfortable pause, "Lieutenant! All clear, but you gotta see this!"

Gray walked through the small frame of the front door where two blood-covered corpses awaited him. The body of a woman lay slumped over that of a man.

"Damn. What do you think?" Gray spoke quietly.

"I don't know, looks bad. Looks like they bled out." Porter leaned closer to inspect the corpses.

"Careful," Gray interrupted, "don't touch 'em. See if there's wires."

"The blood's comin' from their mouths." He looked around the corpses. "No wires."

Two men from outside walked into the room.

Gray turned around as they approached. "Check the back room there. See if there's more. Hand me that stick," he said, pointing to a round wooden rod leaned in the corner.

Gray lifted the woman's chin.

"Oh, man," Porter groaned.

Everyone looked. Large ulcers broke the skin throughout the front of the woman's neck and dried blood covered her chest.

"The man's got the same thing. Oh, God," Gray said. "Do ya'll see any other wounds?"

They looked closely, with no response to the question.

"Okay, let's move. We'll document this, but we've got to move on."

The radio blared in his ear. "Lieutenant. Lieutenant, we need you with A group."

Gray and the others left the house and walked outside into the evening air, where a slight breeze from the west cooled his skin. He looked across the wide dirt path between the buildings.

"I need to see all of the squad. Outside," he said.

"Lieutenant, you better get in here," a voice said from inside the hut across the path.

Gray walked inside and looked down to see a man struggling to breathe, barely conscious. The gaunt man lay on his side embracing two motionless children. Blood oozed from his mouth.

"What do we do with him?"

"I want you out of here. You too, Porter." Gray tapped his arm. "I want everybody out."

Outside is better than inside, Gray thought.

"What do we do about him? He's gonna die if we don't do something."

"We don't know what's happened here. My job is to keep *you* alive, not him. I want everybody out."

They all moved out the door, but could still hear the man on the ground struggling to breathe. Outside, the light slipped away as sunset approached. They saw no signs of life anywhere else.

Gray walked to the end of the dirt path away from the buildings and switched his radio to wide-area broadcast.

"Two-six-five-nine to big eye…two-six-five-nine to big eye, over."

After a brief pause, "Two-six-five-nine, we read five by five. Position clear by GPS. Over."

"Condition is alarming. No enemy. Just civilians. About a hundred. All dead except one. But he'll be dead soon. Bleeding from the mouth. Over."

"*All* dead but one? Did I hear that correctly? Over."

"Affirmative. Preliminary count likely about a hundred. Perhaps chemical weapon used. Internal bleeding, bleeding from mouth, bleeding from skin. Over."

The radio was silent.

Gray spoke again, "No signs of lingering threat. Instructions? Over."

"Hold position. Will call shortly. Maintain position."

Gray wondered what they had found—something terrible.

"Two-six-five-nine. Two-six-five-nine," the radio crackled.

"Two-six-five-nine, here." Gray swallowed hard. "Any instructions?"

"Where were they in their homes?"

"Most were in bed or in chairs. Some were outside, but very few. Over."

After another uncomfortable pause on the radio, the soft static broke again. "Lieutenant you must hold that position. We'll arrange a special extraction. We must arrange decon. Over."

Gray's stomach rolled.

"Roger, two-six-five-nine out."

He knew it was the right decision.

"All groups, back to zero-zero rally point."

They waited outside the village for extraction to decontamination. The extraction team arrived within an hour, and the flight was silent. Gray knew that they were all in trouble.

The tube in Gray's windpipe pressed his esophagus in such a way that he felt the need to swallow. He struggled against the perceived obstruction, but couldn't clear it. He tried to cough, but the searing pain with each breath suppressed any sudden air movement. Thoughts were jumbled, as he drifted in and out of consciousness throughout the day.

"Lieutenant, please relax," the nurse said as he pushed additional lorazepam, a sedative, into the intravenous line in Gray's left hand. "This will help some. Do you understand what I'm saying?"

He nodded.

"We're almost to Ramstein in Germany. They'll be able to do more than we can here in the air."

The endotracheal tube prevented air from moving his vocal cords. Speech was impossible.

"Are you in pain, sir?" the nurse asked.

He nodded again.

"Morphine will help."

He tried to move his right hand, but it was strapped to the gurney.

"Sorry, sir, but we have to keep your hands down—to keep you from pulling the tube out. Just relax. We're trying to help you."

Gray slowly turned to his left and saw Porter next to him, also attached to a ventilator. He looked up to the nurse for an explanation.

"Do you recognize him?" the nurse asked.

He nodded.

"Unfortunately, he and one other are the only ones left. I hate to be the one to tell you this. Nobody else made it to this flight."

Gray stared up at the ceiling of the plane.

"You two are pretty sick yourselves, but we've been successful so far. You stay with us, now. We've come too far for you to check out on us now."

He continued to stare at the ceiling.

"Damn," the nurse said as the telemetry monitor alarm sounded. "Captain, he's bradying down again. Rate's down to forty. Complexes are widening out."

"Push atropine and epi," the captain said as he walked over to the side of the gurney.

"We lost rhythm, sir. He's flatlined."

"Start chest compressions."

The nurse lowered the gurney and placed the palm of his left hand over Gray's sternum with his right hand on top of his left and pressed firmly downward at about eighty times per minute. Advanced cardiac life-support continued for twelve minutes.

Gray continued to stare at the ceiling. Lifeless.

- two -

Joe Mason reached across the table to reach more Rishtaye, a traditional Palestinian dish, but Saida wouldn't let him. Her job was to serve the men. She quickly stood from her place and grabbed the tray to carry it to him.

"I can reach it," Joe said as he stood to meet her halfway.

"She's fine, Joe," Emad said, sitting still at the table.

Joe enjoyed the conversation with his next-door neighbor, Emad Alhaddar. Emad had invited Joe for dinner at his home in Little Rock for just the second time in the nearly three years that they had known each other. They had remained friends ever since sharing difficult night call as interns in the Intensive Care Unit.

Joe knew that the customs were different before he came to dinner. Emad's house was austere, but reasonably well-appointed and organized. The dining room, where they sat, connected to the kitchen through a small doorway. Joe could hear Saida in the kitchen as she cleaned some dishes from the meal. Their two-year-old son had already gone to bed, and they were expecting their second child, a daughter, in three months. Despite pregnancy, she attended to her household duties.

Three months earlier, Joe remembered, the senior resident physician in the Cardiac Care Unit, who was from Syria, became embroiled in controversy when he required the women medical students to walk behind the men during rounds. The staff physician reprimanded him, but the Syrian had made his point— women did not belong, not as doctors, not ahead of men.

"Thank you, Saida. Your food is wonderful," Joe said with a smile as he looked up at her.

She nodded and carried the remaining empty plates to the kitchen. The men continued their conversation.

"It's not as simple as you make it out, Joe," Emad said as he finished the last bite of his bread and yogurt.

"Why not?" Joe said. "I don't see why you guys don't just join up with the Israelis. We don't have little countries here in the United States for each ethnic group."

"That's not right, Joe. When you guys stole the land of the American Indians, you set them up on their own land, with their own sovereignty. That's just the same. That's all we're asking for."

"Okay, good point."

"Listen, man, we Palestinians are giving up a lot in this. We're giving up all claims to the other land, which is still technically ours. I mean, I still have title to land outside of Jerusalem that belonged to my grandfather. He was forced to leave. No payment. Nothing."

"Yeah, but…"

"No...listen, Joe. All I want to do is get our land back. I'm not demanding it back, even though technically it belongs to us. I simply want to buy it back. That's why I'm here in the United States. I'll get my work visa and work wherever I can to earn money. I figure it'll take about six years before I'll have the money to buy the land outright."

"You just want to buy it?"

"Yeah, that's the law there now. Whether I like it or not doesn't matter. That's what it'll take. I just want to get my family's land back. Peacefully."

"I don't know if I could do that," Joe said.

"Sure you could. You'd do what it takes, to take care of your family."

"I don't know, Emad. I haven't had a normal family since I was sixteen years old. I'm pretty selfish now. I just don't know if I could sacrifice myself that much, for that long, just for a piece of land."

"That's not what it is to us, Joe. It's not just a piece of land. It's about home and family. It's about being left alone, to live how we want to live. We need this, Joe. And you'd understand as well if it was happening to you, I promise."

"Maybe you're right," Joe replied. "Maybe I'd view it differently if I had a big family. But, I'm telling you, I'm pretty selfish when it comes right down to it."

"You'd see it differently, Joe. Trust me, you would."

"Yeah, probably. I just want to understand things for what they are. Right or wrong, you know."

"Yeah, I know what you want, but some problems are just too complex to understand in simple terms. Sometimes it's just not so clear."

"No way, Emad. Right is right, and wrong is wrong. It shouldn't be unclear."

"I agree, it shouldn't be, but it is." Emad stood up from the table.

Joe stood as well.

"I appreciate your hospitality, Emad."

"No problem. We'll talk more about this."

"I'd like that," Joe said as he peeked around the doorway into the kitchen. "Thanks again, Saida. I haven't eaten this well in months."

"You're welcome," she said softly. "Come again and visit, especially when we have more." She placed her hand on her pregnant belly.

"Thanks again." Joe laughed.

Emad opened the front door. "I'll see you tomorrow, Joe. Take care not to annoy Dr. Moon tomorrow. He might keep you all the way through the night for rounds."

Joe laughed as he walked out the door.

◆ ◆ ◆

The summer heat the following day was nearly unbearable. Joe remembered again what he didn't like about staying in Arkansas to finish his medical training. Even though the temperature was ninety-four degrees as he walked across the asphalt parking lot, it felt much hotter. The sun baked everything, including him, so he moved swiftly towards the air-conditioning of the Little Rock Veteran's Administration Hospital. He was late once more for afternoon rounds. A long lunch took him fifteen minutes past one o'clock, but he had to finish every bite of his favorite sandwich, the fried oyster po-boy. He was finishing his last few days of his Infectious Diseases rotation, an elective rotation in his third and final year. With four medical students and one first year resident on the team, his temporary absence wouldn't be noticed.

Once in the building, Dr. Sam Bradley, the Chairman of the Medical Service, spotted him. He looked at his watch and shook his head. Joe hated the appearance that he didn't care about the rotation; Infectious Disease held a keen interest for Joe, but he couldn't rush the oyster sandwich.

Joe took one of the back elevators to the fifth floor of the VA so he had less chance of being spotted. He caught up to the rounding team as they left the first patient's room on floor 5D. The staff doctor, Dr. Moon, remained in the room. He hadn't noticed Joe's absence.

"Did I miss anything good, Dave?" Joe said as he walked up slowly behind the team of students and junior residents crowded outside the patient's room.

"You suck, man," said the junior resident, as he rolled his eyes. "You just leave me here with Dr. Moon and the students. Man, you're mean."

"Hey, the sandwich couldn't be rushed. You don't want me to choke, do you?"

"Yeah, I'll choke you myself if you leave me here to fly solo on Moon's rounds."

Joe followed the team of four medical students, two junior residents, and the attending physician, Dr. Moon, into room 501, a four-bed ward with all beds full. Patient privacy was impossible in these rooms, but wasn't expected either.

"Who's this first one?" Joe asked quietly as he glanced at the patient list.

"New consult this morning," the junior resident said. "Forty-two-year-old guy from Bald Knob. A farmer. Came in yesterday to Marty's team—fever, rash, headache, nausea. Was kind of goofy as well, pretty confused."

"Oh, great...I know where we're going with this one," Joe said. "Did the ward team tap him?"

"Yeah, lumbar puncture was done last night. It was okay, a couple of white cells, couple of reds, normal glucose, normal protein."

"Good." He didn't want to endure a procedural instruction from Dr. Moon. Teaching rounds were painful enough.

As Dr. Moon exited the room, he stopped at the sink and washed his hands.

"Here we go," Joe said quietly to the intern. "This guy takes a full sixty-second hand wash out of each room. He's a fanatic."

The intern laughed.

"Have you noticed his hands?"

"Cracked like a dry lake bed. It's gross."

Dr. Moon finished his ritual and turned back to the students.

"Alice, what did you think of the rash?"

"Well, it was red, lacy appearing," she responded with some trepidation. "No bumps, and it was distributed all over the trunk and face."

"What constitutional symptoms did he have?"

"Um, he had some fever initially with chills," she replied with an extended pause. "He also had a pretty bad headache."

"Did you notice anything else important?"

She paused with a strained look on her face. The whole group stared at her as if she were going to reveal the winning lotto numbers.

"No, I didn't notice much else."

"Good. I didn't notice anything else either. Where does all of this information lead you? Alice... I'll let you off the hook."

He looked at the rounding team for his next victim. "Don, what do you think has happened to this patient?"

Don looked down at his feet, as if they would give him some inspiration.

"I really don't know," he finally responded.

"That's okay." Dr. Moon paused. "What question would you ask next?"

After another round with Don looking at his feet and at the wall, Dr. Moon moved on.

"What would be the best next question to ask?"

"Does he have any outside pets?" Joe responded quickly.

Joe knew where all of this questioning was going. As the senior resident on the service, he had been through many such lines of questioning.

"That is exactly what I would ask," beamed Dr. Moon. "Why is that important?"

"Has he had exposure to ticks that may have bitten him?" Joe was confident. "This constellation of findings—the fever, the headache, the characteristic rash, is suggestive of tick fever, such as Ehrlichiosis or Rocky Mountain Spotted Fever."

"Why is that important here? I mean would you think the same thing if we were rounding in Seattle?" asked Dr. Moon.

"No." Joe was quick. "We're in Arkansas, the tick fever capital of the world."

"Joe is exactly right. We must consider all of the possibilities. That's why the patient was started on doxycycline. It'll provide excellent coverage."

After four more hours of incessant questioning by Dr. Moon, hospital rounds mercifully ended. Joe walked up to the sixth floor to talk to the chief of the medical service, Dr. Sam Bradley. Joe had first met him as a second-year medical student when he rotated through Bradley's research laboratory. He visited often; with each visit, he became more of a friend in addition to a mentor.

Joe respected Dr. Bradley for his other contributions as well. He had been Chief at the VA Hospital for the previous twelve years and was a past national president of the American College of Physicians. Joe also admired him for staying in Arkansas, despite multiple job offers outside the area. With the exception of his five-year commitment to the Army in Vietnam, Dr. Bradley had never lived for any extended period away from Arkansas.

"I saw you strolling in from lunch, thirty minutes late," Dr. Bradley said with a laugh.

"Well, I'm rounding with Dr. Moon. I was eating a large lunch because who knew when my next meal would come? We might have been rounding all night," Joe said.

"Say no more." Dr. Bradley smiled. "He certainly takes the slow road to get to the point, but he's a good teacher overall."

"I agree. He's slow but thorough."

"How are things going in your job search?"

"Pretty good. I'd like to head north a bit. All it takes is a brief trip outdoors in the Arkansas heat and humidity for me to want to head to a cooler climate. I've had some promising prospects in Missouri and Iowa and one in Colorado. I'd like to stay in a relatively small town, in a smaller hospital that doesn't have a lot of sub-specialists."

"I hope things go well. You know I can make some calls if you need me to. You also know that you always have a job here. I know we can't pay what you could get out in private practice, but you'd be teaching, which I know you like."

"Thanks again. I appreciate the offer, but I need to get away from the academic scene for a while. Who knows, if I were to stay for a while, I might end up like Dr. Moon. What a scary thought."

Joe laughed at the thought. Dr. Bradley laughed as well.

Joe left the building and began his drive home, which he enjoyed on most days as a way to unwind. He turned off the radio and ignored the traffic. Being alone with the low rumbling noise of the tires on the pavement was relaxing.

His thoughts turned to the weekend. He was scheduled Saturday night for the Emergency Room in Pine Bluff, where he worked about three shifts per month for extra money. The work was hectic at times, but the pay was good. He earned as much money in three shifts as he would make all month with his resident's salary. The other benefit of moonlighting was the complimentary membership to the Pine Bluff Country Club, a reward that the Pine Bluff medical community gave to moonlighting residents to entice them to consider staying in the community to practice full-time. Joe usually volunteered for the Saturday night shift so that he could play golf at the Country Club on Sunday morning.

Joe had started playing golf while in college in Chicago. After playing once with his roommate's father, a Chicago policeman, he had become hooked on the game. He continued to play, and improve, throughout medical school. He liked the public golf courses, removed from the snobbish country club scene, but he also appreciated playing quality courses, which were usually the private ones.

- three -

Joe was busy all night in the ER on that Saturday night shift. Nothing really interesting came through the doors, just the usual: two heart attacks, a diabetic in ketoacidosis, two drug overdoses, three car accidents, and the usual stream of routine colds, aches, and pains that comprised the largest amount of work done in the 'emergency' room setting. The shift ended on a good note when a patient whom he had treated for a heart attack three weeks earlier came back to thank him for 'saving his life.'

The drive over to the golf course was short. The sun was fairly bright for 8:30 a.m. with some early morning haze. The temperature was already eighty-five degrees. Joe parked his eleven-year-old, purple Nissan Altima and checked in at the golf pro shop.

"Morning, Doc."

"Good morning, Bill."

"Saving lives last night?"

"Just like every night."

Bill had been the golf pro at Pine Bluff Country Club for longer than Joe had been alive. He was a crusty, chain-smoking seventy-two-year-old who could whip almost anyone on and off the golf course, and he was particularly feisty after his first scotch and water of the day, which had been ten minutes ago. Joe never hassled him about his drinking and smoking. At Christmas, Joe had bought him an expensive bottle of twelve-year-old Glenmorangie single malt.

"Usual foursome's a bit shy today. I've paired you with some good golfers though."

Joe liked playing with better golfers. Playing faster, he could get home earlier to get some sleep. Because of the job search, he hadn't played or practiced much over the last two months. Lately, his only chance to play was after his Saturday night shift. After a few minutes of warm-up, Joe teed up his ball and promptly hooked it into the fairway bunker. This was going to be a long day on the course, he thought.

◆　◆　◆

As bag after bag went through the conveyor in the Newark airport, Rachel Owanski struggled to keep her concentration on the x-ray monitor screen. Her mind periodically wandered to thoughts of vacation when she would place her own bags on the conveyor belt to be checked as she traveled to Florida to visit her sister.

Her wandering thoughts jolted back to her job as she noticed four small bottles in a bag. She stopped the conveyor to get a better look. At the top of each bottle was a small metal nozzle and cylinder. She pulled the bag from the end of the x-ray unit to search it manually. She wasn't too surprised to see that the bottles were Vidal Sassoon Extra Hold Hair Spray, but when the owner of the bag reached across to claim it she laughed to herself; he was nearly bald. Perhaps all the hairspray was to keep the few remaining hairs glued to his head.

When the balding man aggressively took his bag, the guard at the metal detector turned to look. As the guard walked closer, the man moved quickly away, looking back over his shoulder.

"Is everything alright, Rachel?" the guard said as he watched the man leave.

"Yeah, Morris, I think he was embarrassed that I searched it. He had no less than four bottles of hairspray. Can you believe it?"

"He has about as much use for hairspray as I do," laughed Morris while rubbing his own perfectly shaved head.

Rachel grinned at him.

Morris looked again at the rapidly walking man, who turned to look back. They caught each other's eyes. A bad feeling came over Morris, so he followed the man. After the man looked back again, he began to run. Morris's instincts peaked, so he pursued.

The man sprinted into the men's restroom, about fifty yards down the hall. Morris followed. The restroom was overflowing with travelers oblivious to everything except their own agendas.

"I need everybody to please leave this area... Now!" Morris shouted.

The man stood near the sinks with his bag open, removing the spray bottles.

Morris pulled his gun from its holster. "Stop what you're doing or I *will* shoot." Morris knew his statement was ridiculous; he couldn't shoot someone over some bottles of hairspray.

The man didn't stop. He removed the first bottle from the bag and placed it on the counter. He then slowly repeated the action three more times, seemingly unfazed by Morris's drawn pistol. The man pressed the nozzle on one of the bottles, and as his finger lifted from the nozzle, it continued to release its contents.

"Stop what you're doing or I *will* shoot you," Morris repeated, more confident now that he actually would shoot.

The man looked back at Morris. His dark eyes were completely devoid of emotion as they turned back to the bottles on the countertop. He reached for the second bottle. Morris aimed at the man's knee and fired. The gunshot reverberated inside the confines of the bathroom. Morris heard screams outside as the man crumpled to the floor.

Once the echoes stopped, the only sound was the hissing of the spray from the first bottle.

The man struggled from the floor to return to his remaining work on the bathroom countertop. His hand neared the second bottle. Morris ran over to him and kicked him back to the floor. He placed his knee on the man's chest and aimed his gun at his face. The man stared back with his dark eyes and rose up so that his forehead touched the end of the gun barrel.

"Pull the trigger, sir. We are all dead anyway. Allahu Akbar," the man said in a perfect British accent.

Morris turned away when two more TSA guards entered the bathroom. The man on the floor reached up and forced the trigger back, firing one bullet into the middle of his own forehead. Morris jumped back. He saw the man exhale two short breaths and then stop. His body lay on the cold tile floor with blood streaming from the back of his head and pieces of bone, flesh, and hair coating the wall behind him. Once again, the only sound was the hissing from the first spray bottle.

"I didn't fire," Morris yelled. "He pulled the trigger himself. He wanted to empty these bottles. I don't know what's in them, but he was willing to die to do it. Seal off this room. Don't let anyone in."

A chill shot up Morris's arms with the uncertainty of what was hissing from the bottle. Was it nerve gas? Was it some sort of a bomb? Morris decided not to touch the bottles, concerned that they might explode.

He waited for help, and after what seemed like forever to him, he heard commotion outside as plastic wrap was taped over the doorway.

"What are you doing out there?" he said. His voice cracked.

As he turned to walk out of the room, two men in ventilation suits entered.

"We're sealing off the ventilation, sir," the first man said in a muffled voice. "We'll get you out shortly."

The second man walked over to the counter where the bottles were sitting. The hissing had stopped just moments earlier as the bottle emptied. He carefully placed all four bottles into heavy plastic bags and sealed them with tape. Morris was surprised at the efficiency of these men, as if they knew exactly what had happened.

- four -

The hallway seemed interminably long. The floor shined with military perfection and seemed to reflect noise. Sounds from many people echoed loudly in the halls of the Pentagon. His own strides reflected sound as he jogged to the meeting. Tom Andersly was late, but the extra time was worth the wait—he had the crucial piece of information. He knew that his boss, Steve Hutchins, the Homeland Security Secretary, needed the confirmatory data. They were overdue for a briefing from the President's National Security Advisor.

Tom burst through the door, out of breath. He handed the paper to Mr. Hutchins, who was seated at a table surrounded by three other staff members.

"Slow down, Tom, slow down," Secretary Hutchins said, as he read the page.

"Sorry, sir. But I knew you would want this before the briefing," Tom said with rapid breaths.

"Is this accurate?" asked Hutchins.

"Checked out twice," Tom said. "They ran the sample three times to be sure. They couldn't believe it either. They found traces of the stuff on the outside of the bags...enough to cause problems."

Tom sat next to his boss, satisfied in a job well done. Verification of the data prior to the meeting had proved to be difficult, but given its obvious importance, he had asked for favors to get it done. His boss demanded results, no excuses, just results. Times like this made Tom appreciate why his boss was so adamant. This information, he knew, would change policy at the highest level, so it had to be perfect.

"...we've gathered information, thanks to our CIA friends on the ground. The cultures were moved in at least three different batch shipments from the lab to other sites. They noted that at least one of the sites was inside Baghdad and I think the site was hit last night."

The light from across the room made it difficult to see the projector presentation. Tom motioned to the aide standing against the wall to adjust the blinds. He looked around the room. His boss, Steve Hutchins, was to his left. Peter Denby, the President's National Security Advisor, was farther to the left at the head of the table. Mr. Denby was taller than Tom remembered. On the other side of the table was the Secretary of Defense, Terence Snow, a former Senator, with two Generals sitting to his left. Tom didn't recognize either of them, nor did he recognize the three people in dark suits sitting at the end of the table; he did not know what agency they represented.

"Yes, it was completely destroyed," the Defense Secretary said. "We were able to enter with the First Marines. They secured the site and catalogued the materials. They sent it to Detrick for testing."

"Thanks," the National Security Advisor said. "The other two sites are unknown at this time. We have leads on four possible target locations, but two are under hostile control. One should be hit today, and the other is in Pakistan and should be hit within the next two days. The Pakistanis said we can't participate in the raid, but they've assured us that we'll get a full report as they get it. We told them very little about the cargo, and we also have a man in the Pakistani group who should feed us reliable intel. We're making every effort to ensure that all of the material is taken out of Pakistani hands."

Tom scribbled notes on his yellow legal pad.

"The reason we're all here is because of what has taken place over the last forty-eight hours since the capture of Assam al-Higgadi," the National Security Advisor continued. "You all should have his information in front of you, along with a picture. His face may look familiar to you. He's been linked to the bombing of the *USS Cole* and several attacks inside Iraq."

The projection changed, showing a man of Arabic appearance outside a coffee shop.

"Now remember, he's Jordanian, not Iraqi, and he's very well-connected. As you now know, he was caught entering Newark last Wednesday...he was alone. The search of his bag yielded four small metal cans. This scenario was identical to the one at JFK where the man was shot dead and the TSA guard died. The Newark area was immediately locked down and taped off. The cans were sealed and bagged and sent to the Detrick lab for analysis. Preliminary testing indicated the contents of the cans were the same as the primary lab of Dr. Aziz in Iraq. It was also the same that killed all of the soldiers that entered Al-Qabar village."

"Excuse me, Pete," the Homeland Security Secretary interrupted. "Tom just handed me results from our own Science and Technology division. The PCR results have confirmed that the contamination from the TSA equipment was identical to the primary weapon."

"Is that confirmed, Steve?"

Tom nodded.

"Yes, it's confirmed."

"Well, then, I suspect the Detrick Lab will say the same things. It seems complete now. Understand as well that al-Higgadi isn't talking at all. He's known to be connected to another cell in Paris, but the French lost track of the other members last week." He rolled his eyes. "Intelligence from the Paris cell shows they have a second wave planned."

"Everything's ready with our team," said the Homeland Security Secretary.

"As I reported to the President two weeks ago, we have an enormous security threat with the Paris cell still active. We convened an emergency scientific panel to make recommendations. As you can see in your packet, the outline of the Project includes some very tough work. We're not happy to be forced to make these choices, but the opinion of the Scientific Advisory Panel is that it's the *only* option. We appreciate very much the full cooperation of the staffs here. CIA is managing the offensive response, as we detailed. The President has created a project team to manage our defensive response. All of the information is in your packets."

He turned the projector off.

"The team is headed by a civilian doctor, in coordination with the USAMRIID lab at Fort Detrick, Maryland. The production facility and field lab will be at the Pine Bluff Arsenal in Arkansas, where we've had full cooperation from Defense in conversion. The Arsenal folks aren't new to this work, so they should do fine. For security reasons, the civilian doctor's identity is to be protected. For our purposes he'll be known as Doctor S. He's a former Army doctor, but has been out for many years. We chose him mainly for his prior research work with this bug. He'll control two labs, one inside the Arsenal and one outside, but he will also meet and coordinate the teams at Detrick and in New York. His contact info is in the packet."

The room filled with the sounds of shuffling paper as the group digested the information in front of them.

"Now, this next point must be clear. The nature of this work will be rough, and the President is clear on that fact. It is the opinion of the Advisory team, my opinion, and that of the President that this is our *only* viable defense option. Given the nature of the Project, secrecy is paramount. No doubt, there'll be many who will judge the work negatively. But, as the President told me just prior to this meeting, history will judge the results more than the methods. Are there any questions?"

"What about the containment strategies for this Project inside the United States?"

Tom turned to look in the direction of the three men at the end of table. He still didn't recognize any of them.

"Excuse me?" Mr. Denby said.

"Yeah. What about containment *inside* the US? This Project team for the defensive response will have tough work. Many will question it. We can't just hope that it'll remain contained without some leaks. What's the strategy for containment?"

"Look," Mr. Denby said rapidly, "we know your people's objections. We've listened to them before, but this is just the only viable option we have. The President has…"

The man interrupted, "What about the Macke Strategy? We presented this in full to the…"

Tom noticed that the man had a large scar above his right eye. Perhaps a shrapnel wound, he thought.

"Again, we've heard all the alternatives," Mr. Denby interrupted again more forcefully, "and the President has made a decision and expects full cooperation from the team—inside this room and outside this room."

The man was silent. The room was silent.

"Fine, then." He stood up from his chair. "We'll plan to meet here every other Wednesday at this time. My staff will send twice-weekly updates, and I'm always available if needed. Thanks."

♦　♦　♦

The harsh fluorescent lights cast flat white light on the papers scattered across the conference room table. The nondescript office was like any other low-level office in America with the smell of burning coffee lingering faintly in the air. After reviewing the reports, the doctor looked out the window and remembered again why he hated New York. His concentration waned as the sounds of the city outside the window interrupted meaningful thought. He knew that most locals either didn't notice it or couldn't do without it, but to him, it was just annoying. After nearly two hours of reviewing reports, he pushed away from the table and stood up to stretch his legs.

He looked down again at the photographic negatives. Dark bands lined up in perfect columns with each band indicating different sized DNA fragments in the electrophoretic gel. The match was unmistakable; the DNA in both samples was the same, which meant that the organisms from which the DNA had been extracted were the same strain. He felt tenseness in his stomach, as the noise outside seemed less noticeable. The knock on the door startled him.

"Yeah," he grumbled. "Come in."

A tall man entered with another behind him. The two men were young and well-groomed, both wearing conservative suits. One face was familiar, but he couldn't remember the man's name. He was terrible at remembering names. He scanned his memory.

"Doctor S, have you had enough time to review the data?" the tall man asked.

"Yeah. The PCR analysis is conclusive. It's the same strain. How long did you say the guard lasted?"

"He died after about eighty-four hours, same as the others. There were two other men just outside the room, but only one of them got sick. He died after only sixty-four hours. The room was contained per Protocol F-21 without problems. I know you probably haven't had time to review the specific isolation protocols, but they've worked well so far."

"I trust that the protocols are effective. Were all four cans positive?"

"Yes, sir. All four cans, sir."

He rubbed his chin. "What about in Newark? Do you have the PCR films from there?"

"No, sir. They're en route."

"And have these from New York been compared to the ones from Dallas and Atlanta?"

"Yes, sir. All the same…to our eyes. But we'd like your opinion."

"Damn. It's not going to stop. I have to get these samples to the team. Please relay all of this information to the General. And tell him I agree with your analysis, and I'll call him myself when I get back to Arkansas. My compliments to your team for acting so quickly. They definitely saved lives."

"Thank you, sir. We're still fully deployed as planned."

Doctor S had great confidence in these men as their management experience had kept the small attacks on Newark, Dallas, Atlanta, and now New York contained. The general public was still unaware, which enabled the team to continue their important work.

- five -

The layout of the Emergency Room in Pine Bluff formed a large rectangle, with trauma rooms to the left, monitored beds in front, and minor medical beds to the right side. The staff, nurses, doctors, and paramedics worked around and inside the center. It functioned well for efficiency.

The usual 2 a.m. slowdown didn't come. The nurse tossed Joe two charts.

"Take the one in Bed 3A first. He looks the worst. They both look bad, though."

"Where'd they come from? Says here in the chart they were picked up on the side of the road."

"They were on the highway towards Rison, about twenty-five miles away, clinging to each other. Neither would speak to the woman who found them. She thought they looked bad, so she helped them into the back of her truck and brought them here."

"Where is she?"

"She left about fifteen minutes ago. She gave a statement to Barney Fife over there and then left."

"You don't like the security guy, Carol?"

"Hell no, not since he let go of that meth addict last weekend. We were trying to restrain him to get him sedated, but Barney Fife let go. Damn guy broke my nose."

"3A you say."

"Yeah, John Doe 1 is in 3A. The other one's in Bed 4."

Joe entered the exam room with his best 2 a.m. smile. The patient was a young white man, fairly thin, wearing filthy overalls and nothing else. He reeked of urine, and the front of his overalls had some fresh bloodstains. The tattoo on his right arm caught Joe's attention. It appeared to be fairly new and definitely homemade. Joe used it as his entry point.

"Did you do your own tattoo there?" pointing to the patient's arm.

"Naw," the man said timidly.

"Who did it? It looks new."

Joe noted that the margins of the tattoo were still quite distinct. He knew that most prison tattoos were made using ink from ballpoint pens. Over time, the ink diffused some in the skin, which caused the margins to blur.

"Dude did it las' month."

"Where do you live?"

"Nowhere."

"You're homeless?"

"Sort ah."

"What do you mean sort of? Where'd you sleep last night?"

"Las' night I slep' in da' fields."

"What about the night before?"

After an uncomfortable pause, he replied, "Anythin' I tell ya is our secret, right?"

"Absolutely. Everything's between you and me."

"They're killin' us."

"What?…what do you mean?"

"Promise me ya won't send me back."

"I promise. Who's doing the killing?"

"The warden, the guards, all of 'em. Took us from our cells to the bad place."

Joe's mind raced. The tattoo was a prison tattoo; the man's overalls were prison issue.

"Why'd you call it the bad place?"

"'Cuz that's where they took us to kill us. Me and Tommy's all that's left from the ten that was taken." He coughed. "We knew we's sick too, so we got out. That lady brung us here. Me and Tommy knew we'd be alright if we'd just get to a real doc." He coughed harder, producing a small amount of blood.

"Why do you think they were trying to kill you?" Joe handed him a tissue.

"Cuz they made us breathe bad air. Three dudes died, and the docs didn't do nothin'. We knew we had to get outta there. I hit the guard with the bed rail. Tommy grabbed the doc and held a needle to his throat. We took the guards' guns and locked 'em in the room with their handcuffs. Then we ran outside. I dunno where we was, but we just kept runnin' until we saw cars. That's when the lady picked us up."

"How long have you been sick?"

"'Bout four days, maybe five."

"What kind of sickness? I see you're coughing up blood."

"Yeah, it's gettin' worse. Breathin's gettin' hard too. Had some chills."

"What about Tommy over there, same stuff?"

"Yeah."

Carol ripped the curtain back. "Dr. Mason. You're needed in Four."

Joe moved quickly to the next room. The respiratory technician squeezed breaths through a resuscitation bag into the second prisoner. Joe looked up at a flat line on the telemetry heart monitor.

"No pulse, doc."

"Okay, prepare to intubate," Joe said as he put on gloves and mask with eye-guards. "Start CPR. I need a large Miller blade and suction set up. Do we have an IV?"

"Yeah, I started an eighteen gauge in his left arm," said the nurse as she gave chest compressions.

"Somebody start another in the right arm. Let's give epinephrine and atropine. I'll intubate with a size eight ET tube."

Joe intubated the patient quickly. After two breaths, the endotracheal tube filled with blood from the lungs.

"Well, I guess pulmonary hemorrhage is the obvious first problem," Joe said loudly. "Go ahead and give the second round of epinephrine and atropine."

The team worked smoothly through the advanced cardiac life support protocol for the next nine minutes, but the patient never regained heart rhythm or breathing.

"Any objections to calling it quits?" Joe asked, knowing that there were none. "Okay, time of death is 2:21."

Joe removed his latex gloves, which were covered in blood, and threw them in the biohazard bag. He left the room to wash his hands but stopped when he caught the eye of the first prisoner through the curtain. He walked back into the room.

"Tommy just died," Joe said quietly.

The first prisoner said nothing. He turned his head and stared at the wall.

"I need to know everything that happened to the two of you."

The patient said nothing.

"If you don't talk to me, I can't help you. I don't want a repeat of what just happened to Tommy."

The first prisoner remained quiet.

"Please," Joe pleaded, "talk to me so I can help."

"You're no different from the rest of 'em. You just want me dead."

"Look, that's not true. I don't know what's happened to you two guys, but it's obvious that you're sick. Whether you just got sick or somebody has made you sick doesn't really matter right now. I need to know what's happened so I can help you."

"Fuck you."

Joe frowned. "Look, man, we can sit here all night if you like, but I *will* find out what's been going on."

The man continued to stare at the wall.

"Fine. But I'll at least tell you what I have to do. The nurse will come back and start you on some medicine that should help. We'll draw some blood to see how your lungs are doing. I'm then going to call another doctor who'll take care of you in the hospital here."

The prisoner said nothing.

"Okay." Joe walked out to the nurse's station. "Carol, can we get an ABG on the Doe in 3A, please?"

"Sure, I'll tell respiratory. He's still at bed four, finishing up."

Joe scribbled parts of the prisoner's story into the ER chart. It seemed ridiculous to him, but certainly it wasn't the strangest story he had heard in his many shifts working in the Emergency Room. He reviewed the labs already done. Chemistries were bad, high creatinine, which meant kidney failure, low bicarbonate with elevated anion gap, which meant metabolic acidosis, high white blood cell count with left shift, which meant infection.

Joe walked over to the radiology reading room. All films from ER patients were placed on one reading board that rotated films according to bed number. He turned to bed four first, those of the prisoner who had died. The film showed fluffy white patches throughout both lungs, with fluid accumulating in both bases. He rotated the machine to bed three, from the first prisoner, who was still alive. It looked nearly identical to Joe. Both men had significant pneumonia. But typical pneumonia didn't cause such massive hemorrhage from the lungs.

"Dr. Mason," Carol called from the desk, "we've got your blood gases from 3A."

Joe walked out to the desk.

"Okay," Carol continued, "pH 7.15, pCO2 63, pO2 61...that's on six liters nasal cannula."

"Damn. That guy's gonna end up tubed as well," Joe said.

"Yep. Hey, good news, though. Dr. Skilton is on unassigned call."

"Oh, great. He's an ass. He won't do shit for this guy."

"Sorry." Carol put the chart into the rack. "Can't help you there."

Joe picked up the phone to call Dr. Skilton. He knew it would be an unpleasant experience explaining this case to him at 2:30 a.m., especially because the patient was too sick to send to a room and wait for morning rounds. Dr. Skilton would have to get out of bed and come see the patient.

The remainder of Joe's night was quiet. He slept from 4:30 until 6:15 in the trauma room. No new patients came into the ER during the shift. He awoke somewhat refreshed. He had learned over time to work efficiently on short rounds of sleep. He jumped down off the trauma table and put his lab coat back on. The lights above the nurses' station seemed brighter as he left the darkened room.

"Hey, Carol, how'd our friendly prisoner make out upstairs?" Joe asked as he walked towards the sliding doors to the parking lot.

"He died at about 5:30. Code Blue was called about then. Dr. Skilton was upstairs with him, so we didn't wake you. Looked like pulmonary hemorrhage, just like John Doe 2."

Joe stopped just short of the door and paused, stunned. Even though he had seen a lot of patients die, he was still quite surprised that both prisoners died so suddenly and in the same unusual way.

"Really? Did Skilton add anything?"

"Nope, just coded the guy."

"Thanks, Carol, see you in two weeks," Joe said. "Hey, if you don't mind, I'll call you in a couple of days when the autopsy reports are done. I'm really curious."

"No problem. See you later, Dr. Mason."

Carol picked up the phone and paused briefly to consider what she was doing. She knew that this call obviously violated patient confidentiality, but she had been promised that it was important. She dialed the number.

"Hello," a tired female voice answered.

"This is Carol from Pine Bluff. You came to see me last week. You told me to watch for strange medical cases from the prison."

"Yes," she replied quickly. "Did you get something?"

"Yeah. Two men came in last night...found on a road between Pine Bluff and Rison. Said they'd escaped from a facility after being taken from Cummins Prison."

"Where are they now? I need to talk to them."

"That's the problem...they're in the morgue."

"What?"

"Yeah, they both died right after they got here."

"You're sure they came from the prison?"

"That's what they said. They told the doc here that the people at the prison made them sick...just like you said."

"Carol, thanks for calling me. I know you're not comfortable with all of this, but I promise, what you've done is a good thing. We need to find out what's going on."

"No problem. Let me know what you find."

"I will. Who was the doctor?"

"The doc's name is Joe Mason. He's from Little Rock...a resident at the Med Center there. He just moonlights down here a few shifts a month. Pretty good guy."

"Thanks, Carol. Call me if you need anything else. You have my number."

"You're welcome. What did you say your name was?"

"Jules Green."

- SIX -

Monday morning comes too early, Joe thought; he was unusually tired from his Saturday night shift. The more he thought about the prisoners, the more questions arose. Why did they die? What killed them? Did somebody deliberately kill them as the prisoner thought? The more Joe thought about the men in a less sleep-deprived state, the more the whole situation bothered him.

Joe called Dr. Jedediah Wethers, a pathologist at the Pine Bluff hospital. He had first met Dr. Wethers when he had visited during medical school. He learned that Dr. Wethers had trained in the late 1940's in Memphis, and he had been the first African-American pathologist in the state of Arkansas. His age had taken a toll on the quality of his work, but he was still very good when he needed to be.

After ten rings on the phone, somebody finally answered in the pathology department and connected him to the physician's office.

"Hello, I'm Dr. Mason. I worked in the ER on Saturday night. There were two men who died and should have had autopsies done. I wanted to see what the results were."

"What was your name again, son?"

Joe was annoyed at being called 'son'. "Dr. Joe Mason."

"Ah, yes, Dr. Mason. I remember you. We played golf three weeks ago. You beat me pretty badly."

"Oh, yes. I hope you're not mad at me," Joe bluffed.

"On the contrary, son. I always enjoy watching someone successfully hit that damn little white ball."

"As much as I'd like to talk golf, sir, I need to get the information from the autopsies, if possible."

"I'm sorry, son. What did you say the name was?"

"Well, that's interesting, too. I don't know their names. They came into the ER as John Does 1 and 2."

"Of course…those men just left this morning."

"What do you mean they left?"

"A couple of people came to claim the bodies. They said the men were prisoners who had escaped from Cummins. They had forms signed from the men's families saying that they didn't want an autopsy done."

"But don't you have to do an autopsy? I thought that since they died within twenty-four hours, or is it forty-eight hours, of admission, that the case would be referred to the coroner automatically."

"Yes, son, you're right. But it's the coroner's option. He's not obligated to order an autopsy unless the circumstances dictate. We told the coroner that the men likely died of pneumonia. So the coroner released them."

Joe remembered that he hadn't included all of the prisoner's story in his own written reports.

"How did the prison get releases so quickly?" Joe asked.

"I don't know, son. I don't work for the prison. Why do you ask?"

"Oh, it's just they had some pretty wild claims about the prison. Their story, plus how quickly they died, just made me curious."

"Well, son, I'll tell you. You can't let curiosity kill you. When you've been around as long as I have, you learn to accept that there's just a lot of things you'll never know."

"I know, Dr. Wethers, but it was just some pretty impressive blood loss from the lungs. Whatever they had was pretty bad."

"No doubt, son, no doubt."

"Dr. Wethers, do you still have the endotracheal tubes from the men? They didn't take them too, did they?"

"I doubt you can culture them, son. The fluids are dried."

"I know, but I have a friend who can do some DNA analysis. It may show something."

"Boy, you're eager. I'll give you that. Let me have a look to see if we still have them."

After a few minutes that seemed like forever to Joe, Dr. Wethers picked up the phone again.

"You're in luck. I've got them both."

"Great. If you'll bag them, I'll come by in the next day or two and pick them up."

"No problem, son. I'll see you on the golf course."

"Thanks. I hope so."

Joe hated being called 'son.'

◆ ◆ ◆

Doctor S drove down the dirt road to the isolated but large building. The design works well, he thought, both for its appearance on the outside as a simple farm building and on the inside as an advanced molecular biology and pathology laboratory. He drove around the building to the large parking area in the back, out of sight from the road a quarter mile to the south. As he entered the building, his secretary greeted him.

"Hello, Doctor. Mr. Moore is here to give you a full update," she said, handing him his daily schedule summary. "Your meeting in New York has been moved back to 3:30 today so the flight will leave an hour later. You'll still be back by 8:00 tonight. They assured me that the facility tour will be brief."

"Thanks. Tell Mr. Moore I'll see him in the small conference room. I need to get some coffee."

"I've already taken care of that, Doctor. It's in the room waiting for you."

"Thanks, Grace."

He walked to the conference room where Mr. Moore was waiting. The windows in the room provided a view of the dense trees near the back of the property. The colors of the leaves contrasted with the dull industrial colors in the room.

"Excellent, I see that you have the latest of the reports," Mr. Moore said as he closed the door. "I've prepared your full packet in the order you requested, sir. I've also got some PowerPoint slides to show as well. Would you mind if my senior staff joined us?"

"Not at all," Doctor S said as he sat at the table.

"Grace," Moore said as he pressed the conference call button, "can you send my staff in, please?" He turned back to the projector. "We'll go ahead and get started. I'm just going to start from the genetics section. I think it makes more sense from there."

"Sure. That's fine." Doctor S leaned back in the chair.

"The automated sequencers ran non-stop for eleven days with the full genome. The modified stair-step technique worked well. It's based on the Venter shotgun technique, as you probably know."

Doctor S nodded.

"The genome consists of just over two thousand three hundred genes. This particular strain was modified to include eight additional genes encoding drug resistance and fourteen genes for the capsule. We think the capsule genes were adapted from the pneumococcus, but that is not yet confirmed."

The door opened and two men and a woman entered and sat at the table opposite Doctor S, but they said nothing.

"We loaded the genome into the analytic database for protein sequencing. The protein work was automated and passed through the sequencers in just seven days. We completed skin and agglutination testing in three days to give us our twenty-two protein candidates."

"What sizes are the proteins?"

"They range in size between thirty to ninety kilodaltons."

"Can we manufacture them quickly?"

"Yes, sir. We should be okay. We've been using ProtCo out of Berkeley with no problems. They have excellent capacity and turnaround time. We've been checking the sample purity here with our sequencers. It's good."

"Let me know if we have any issues that could be a problem when we ramp up production."

"I understand, sir. I'll let you know if we see problems."

Moore advanced to the next slide.

"Now, we've narrowed our scope to twenty-two proteins for immunology. Of these, we think eleven are the best candidates based on expression and ease of use. We're moving forward into Phase Two testing with these eleven."

"Are they all extracapsular?"

"No, sir. Nine are extracapsular and two are intracellular. It wouldn't surprise me if the intracellular ones are excluded quickly, given my previous experience."

"I agree."

"We're giving these candidates to the delivery team for testing across techniques."

"I set up three different delivery techniques, Mr. Moore."

"Yes, sir. And I agree completely with your choices. I think when you combine ease of manufacture and delivery, your selections are ideal. Now, we've divided the subjects into three groups, separating the techniques. Each one will get divided into three subgroups for mucosal, skin, and intramuscular inoculation. We're set up to measure the specific IgM, IgA, and IgG immune responses quantitatively and sequentially. We'll extend the data across subjects to average the responses, and we should have that data by next Friday, sir."

"Excellent work, Mr. Moore. I don't think I have anything to add." Doctor S looked across the table to the other team members. "Your work is appreciated, too. I know you've all had to leave your jobs and your families to be here, but your work is important."

"Yes, sir," they said in unison.

"Mr. Moore, do you have anything else?"

"Yes, sir, one more thing. We're also going to monitor response across HLA genetic groups as well. We may have some variability across those groups. I want to ensure that we get our best result for all subjects, not just our best average."

"Excellent. Let me know if you need anything from me. Continue your work."

Doctor S walked out of the conference room and down the short hallway to his office. Grace looked up from her desk as he approached.

"Grace, I need copies of all of this work to be sent to Dr. Henderson, please. He needs to review it. Tell him that we'll get together next week to discuss it. Can you set that up?"

"Yes, sir. No problem. Don't forget about your conference call."

"Oh, yeah. That's at ten-thirty, right?"

"Yes, sir. I'll call you in your office when they're ready."

"Thanks Grace. Don't forget. Dr. Henderson will need his full briefing before Wednesday. After that, I'll get him set up both here and at the Arsenal," Doctor S said as he walked into his office.

The conference call with the Defense Secretary was brief. The Department of Defense efficiently converted the Pine Bluff Arsenal to include the Project additions. Doctor S had no outstanding issues with the conversion; he mostly wanted to thank the Secretary for his efforts. He knew that the hardest work was ahead.

- seven -

The e-mail was delivered, as usual, to the Yahoo account. It contained very little information, just a name, three digital pictures, and three contact addresses. The first payment had already been deposited into the numbered account in Bern, Switzerland. Bern was home: a cosmopolitan European city where anonymity was easy.

He wrote a single line reply. "To be done. Mercury."

The final line of the e-mail gave the time frame—three weeks, not much time for the job. He had to travel, find the target, follow it, and deduce the routine. He had to obtain clean weapons, untraceable. Nothing unusual, but it took time and money.

With acceptance of the job, the second payment was deposited. The third and final payment would come after completion of the job. This was how he worked, and he was the best in the world. Nobody knew who Mercury was, not even what he looked like; and few people even knew how to contact him for jobs. The CIA was his best and most frequent customer, with seventeen jobs over the last ten years.

The target appeared to be of Arabic lineage, last reported to be in Washington, DC. The street name and apartment number were unfamiliar but could be located easily. He didn't care so much exactly where the target was from, except when it mattered for the purpose of stalking him.

The airplane ride was long, non-stop from Munich, Germany, to Atlanta, Georgia. He dressed in an Armani suit, carried a briefcase and an American passport; he looked and acted like a business executive. He leaned toward the attractive young lady next to him to pass the time with conversation.

"Where are you traveling?" he asked, noticing the woman's tan legs extending from her skirt.

"I live in Atlanta, at least in the area. I've been in Nice, France on a photo shoot."

"Are you a photographer?"

"No, I'm a model. The photographs were for *Glamour* magazine. My agent says there's a good chance I'll make the cover."

"Congratulations."

He looked down at her breasts and thought that she was very likely to make the cover.

"They're pretty nice, aren't they?"

"Excuse me?" he replied, trying not to show his surprise.

"My breasts. You were looking at my breasts." She smiled. "It's okay. They've given me a good job that allows me to travel. I don't mind people staring. I just hope that my looks can keep me employed for a few more years. I'm thirty-three years old, which is old for models. I hope I didn't embarrass you."

"Oh, no. I'm not embarrassed. And the answer to your first question is a definite yes. They're very nice."

She blushed as her flirting was returned.

"What do you do for a living?" she asked.

Professional assassin.

He wanted to tell the truth, just to see the response. However, he continued the charade.

"I'm a bond trader with Merrill Lynch and was in Munich exploring some international opportunities. It's actually a pretty interesting job. Well, not as glamorous as modeling, but then what is?"

"I'll bet you make a lot of money."

"Well, I make enough to fly first-class, but the really big money is made by the underwriters, you know, the people who actually arrange the original bonds themselves. I'm just a glorified middleman, but I like it."

"I'm Kathryn Staley," she said extending her hand. "I didn't catch your name."

"Mark Goodman. Nice to meet you."

They shook hands and held the grip for a bit longer than typical.

"Are you married?" Mercury asked.

"No, I've been divorced for about three years. My husband only loved my breasts...and those of others. He had no appreciation for my work, nor any patience for my traveling. He was also very jealous. I couldn't handle it for very long, so I left. What about you? Is there a Mrs. Goodman?"

"No. I've been too wrapped up in my work. I know I need to slow down, but I find the slow lane a bit boring."

"Do you think you'll ever slow down?" she asked while stroking her right knee. "I mean what good is all the money if you don't use it to enjoy yourself?"

"I'm sure that when I find something that interests me more, I'll have no problem changing gears a bit."

He noticed that as she stroked her leg, her skirt migrated farther up, revealing more of her legs.

After landing, the two continued their conversation in the airport bar, which led to a long cab ride to the woman's condominium in an Atlanta suburb. The conversations led to kissing and then to the point that Mercury could tell that her breasts were created not by birth but by a clever plastic surgeon.

Mercury left the next morning without waking her. He was late in getting to Washington, DC, but he considered the little detour to be worth the extra effort. He traveled by car for the rest of his trip, which separated the job from the flight—airplane tickets are easily traced and monitored. And the trip gave him time to think as he drove.

He arrived in Washington shortly after dark and checked into the Ritz-Carlton. He loved posh hotels—the appearance, the accommodations, and the service. He settled into his luxurious bed for a restful night's sleep. The next day would prove to be quite busy.

After a light continental breakfast and dark coffee, he set out to stalk his prey. He took a cab ride to Rodman Street, just west of 47th. It was plain, with townhouses lining both sides. His outward appearance was different, now with gray hair and a beard, and an extra thirty pounds of weight. People were walking on both sides of the street, which made blending into the crowd quite easy while he observed the movements of the target into and out of his apartment. This job will be easy, he thought.

The Arabic man spent most of his time in the apartment on the second floor. He came outside each night at about six o'clock to walk down the street to eat dinner at a Pakistani Restaurant. Mercury didn't know what he was doing in the apartment, and he really didn't care, concerned only with completing the job.

The following day, Mercury dressed in khaki pants and yellow polo shirt and drove around southeast Washington, DC. The neighborhood wasn't the typical place for a white man dressed in khakis and polo shirt; he wanted to attract attention, driving a green Ford Minivan. He pulled to the side of the road and exited the car with a map, as if he were a lost traveler in the wrong part of town. It didn't take long: two young men came to 'help.'

"You lost, man?" The older one asked.

"Yeah, sort of," Mercury replied. "I need some help but not with finding my way. I need to hire somebody for a job. It's really easy money."

"We're listening. What do we gotta do, kill someone?" the man laughed.

"Oh no, nothing like that. I just need to get somebody's wallet. I can't take it myself. He'll recognize me. I really need to get it. What'll it cost me to hire you to do it?"

"Just take the guy's wallet. That's it?" the older one looked at the other and smiled.

"That'll cost five hundred."

"No problem."

"That's five hundred each, and whatever cash is in the wallet belongs to us."

"No problem. I'll pick you up at five tonight."

"What do you need the wallet for, man?"

"I'd rather keep it to myself. I just need you for the job."

He drove to Baltimore to get the two .357 revolvers that he had arranged earlier to get. He particularly liked his contact there, as he always delivered a clean product, and on time. Best of all, he never asked questions.

Shortly before 5 p.m., he picked up the two unsuspecting thieves. They drove towards the apartment, and he showed them the front door where the Arabic man would soon exit. He showed them a picture as well so that they would recognize him.

Once Mercury dropped the two men off in front of the apartment, he circled the block, parked on the street just down from the apartment and watched. At 5:55, the Arabic man walked out the front door as expected. The Hispanic boy approached him from the front and bumped him as he went by. As the Arabic man turned to look back, the other boy grabbed him from behind.

Mercury pulled forward in his car. As he pulled alongside the scene, all three men looked at him as he raised the gun. He fired the first shot through the temple of the Arabic man and his body fell limply to the ground. The two boys stood still, stunned. He unloaded the remaining eleven bullets into them and then sped away.

He posed as a newspaper photographer to allow himself to get the necessary photographs, verification that secured the third and final payment for a successful job. Once again, he did not know, or care, who the victim was.

He took the digital photo and uploaded it into his laptop computer as the taxi approached a Starbuck's coffee shop along Pennsylvania Avenue, just three blocks from the White House. The wireless network signal was strong, extending out into the street.

"Stop here in front of the Starbuck's," Mercury said. "I want to swing in and grab a cup."

"Sure thing," the driver said as he parked along the curb.

He then sent the photo with the text, "Job completed. Mercury."

"Hey, you want a cup?"

"Sure thing. Just black. Thanks."

After less than five minutes, Mercury returned to the cab and slid across the seat, handing the coffee forward to the driver.

"Thanks," said the driver with a smile.

"Can we wait here for a minute? I want to get something else off their Internet access."

"Sure thing, just tell me when to go."

Mercury checked his online bank account where he received confirmation of the deposit. He changed web pages to his bank in Bern, Switzerland, and arranged for the balance to be transferred via anonymous bearer bonds to his full account.

Outstanding.

This deposit took his final total over forty-eight million dollars.

◆ ◆ ◆

The cubicle opened to the entire room, which made Hayden a bit uncomfortable. He liked some privacy when he worked, but his boss said that the hierarchical form of most offices was counterproductive; he thought that everyone should be more equal. From secretaries to the boss himself, everyone had essentially the same space, and lack of privacy.

Hayden didn't care much for the vagaries of the modern office; he just wanted a private workspace so he could listen in peace to the Cubs game over the Internet as they played the Cardinals. Just as the fifth inning ended, his screen showed an e-mail alert. It was from Mercury, so he opened it immediately.

Even though he could never participate directly in planning such a contract, he did take a macabre interest in the pictures that he reviewed. These pictures were no exception; he could plainly recognize the face of Ali Al-Sharif, with the obvious gunshot wound to the temple. He looked closely at the lifeless half-open eyes.

Hayden raised his head above the cubicle wall.

"Mr. Cahill. We have verification."

The department had previously conducted twenty-six successful hits for the Project—Al-Sharif was number twenty-seven. The reports said that he had been helping to direct intelligence gathering for the al-Qaeda in the Washington, DC area, and his elimination would hamper their efforts tremendously. Mercury was used for the job because it had to be done in a way that would arouse the least investigation, but public enough to be an example to other operatives.

Mr. Cahill peered at the screen. It was unmistakable; Al-Sharif had been neutralized.

"Has the money been sent?" he asked.

"Yes, sir. It was wired in the usual fashion."

"Any trace on Mercury?"

"No, sir. He's still just a ghost. The money was taken and the account is already closed."

"I'll notify the team." Mr. Cahill turned to leave the cubicle. "And Hayden, by the way, are the Cubs still winning?"

Hayden blushed. "No, sir. A two out double scored two runs last inning."

- eight -

The resident's lounge at the University Hospital was distant—a long walk through narrow hallways to a remote outside corner of the building. Joe thought it had been put there to discourage the resident physicians from using it; they were supposed to be working, or so they were told. The room was dirty, with two stained couches, a vinyl-covered recliner stolen from one of the patient rooms, and a Formica-covered table that was still sticky from yesterday's orange juice.

"Are these rolls safe?" Joe asked, looking at the two interns sitting on the couch.

"Yeah, they're from today. Drug reps were here earlier."

Joe grabbed a plastic knife and cut the cinnamon roll in half.

"Hey, Joe?" the intern said.

"Yeah, Marty?"

"We're going over our stuff for the ventilators. We've got rounds with Dr. Hilman in twenty minutes. You know how he is about the vents—gotta know the damn physics of the things."

"Yeah, I remember. It's okay. What's the question?"

Joe sat in the vinyl recliner.

"Okay, I understand the peak pressure stuff and compliance, but I'm still not clear on the plateau pressure."

"Yeah, Marty, no problem. The plateau pressure tells you what the pressure is in the alveoli, you know, alveolar pressure. Several things contribute to it, and it's a good number to know. Peak pressure can change with just about anything— secretions, peak flow, tidal volume. Plateau tells you what's going on down low. If it jumps up, then you need to know what's going on. Remember, it's a static measurement, no flow. Pressures equalize throughout the system."

"Alright, I see. That's why you program the pause on the vent. To get a static measurement."

Emad Alhaddar walked into the lounge and peered into the sweet roll box. "These good, Joe?"

"Yeah, not as good as Oyster Bar, but good." Joe looked back to the intern. "Right. I had a guy last month who popped an emphysema bleb. Boom. Instant tension pneumothorax. We didn't know anything, just saw him struggling all of a sudden and his blood pressure dropped to seventy. I set the inspiratory pause and measured plateau pressure. It had doubled, which meant that we were ventilating half the space. There's your diagnosis. He had crappy breath sounds anyway, with his emphysema, so auscultation wasn't as helpful."

"Got it. Thanks." The intern looked back to his paper.

"What's up, Emad?" Joe asked.

"I need something for my stomach. I've got rounds in ten minutes."

"Hey, I was working the ER in Pine Bluff and had a weird couple of cases."

"What do you mean, weird?" Emad sat on the couch next to the interns.

"Couple of escaped prisoners. They said they were deliberately infected at the prison."

"I'd say that's weird," Emad said, taking a bite.

"Anyway, both of them died right after getting to the ER."

"Oh, man. What'd they have?"

"I don't know. One guy coded and died almost as soon as he got there. The other guy died after about four hours. Both had high fever and pulmonary hemorrhage."

"They died of pulmonary hemorrhage?"

"Yeah, that's what it looked like"

"Ouch, that'd suck."

"It did. Anyway, I called back to pathology there to see what they found on post mortem, but they said none was done. Said the families came to claim the bodies."

"Well…?" Emad said as he took another bite of his sweet roll.

"Well, both guys came in as John Does, said they were poisoned by the prison, died damn near as soon as they got there. No autopsy was done and the bodies were claimed by family within a couple more hours. Just seems really fishy to me."

"Why do you care, Joe?" the intern said, interrupting the story. "You're almost out of here, done with all of this. Just let it go. They're just prisoners, man."

"Well, I'd be curious, too," Emad said. "What are you going to do?"

"I'm getting the ET tubes with the dried secretions to see what I can find. I thought about sending them to Brad Yates. You remember him?"

"Yeah, I think so. He came down to stay with you a couple of times. The guy up in Maryland at NIH, right?"

"That's him. He's done some DNA work for bacterial diagnosis. I thought he could maybe analyze the secretions."

"That should work, Joe. Unless it's viral."

"It sure looked bacterial to me. I'm just really curious about the whole thing. It was pretty bizarre."

The intern stood up from the couch. "I'd just let it go and move on. Sounds like a lot of work."

Emad rolled his eyes.

"Yes, the American work ethic...I'm so proud," Joe laughed.

"Seriously, Joe," Emad said, "I'd keep looking. Maybe the prisoners were right. Maybe somebody's doing something they shouldn't down there at the prison. We had a similar thing happen in Ramallah. The Mossad was taking young prisoners from the jail there and testing torture techniques."

"I don't know, Emad. I think that'd be pretty hard to keep quiet here."

"Just remember, Joe. You Americans trained the Mossad in Israel."

Joe was silent.

"Sorry, Joe, but don't forget that sometimes it's not as clearly right or wrong as you want it to be."

"I'll remember," Joe said as he stood up from the recliner. "Ya'll be good, and don't let Dr. Hilman give you any crap."

"Thanks, Joe," the intern said, reviewing his notes.

Joe left the lounge and walked through the maze of hallways to get back to the hospital stairwell. As he approached the stairs, a young woman walked towards the door. She wore a gray business suit with a white blouse, unusual for this area of the hospital.

"Can I help you?" Joe offered.

"Thanks," she said, looking at Joe's nametag. "But I think I found what I'm looking for."

Joe opened the door, and they both walked into the stairwell.

"What do you mean?" Joe asked.

"You."

"Huh?"

"I was looking for you."

They paused inside the stairwell, opposite each other. Joe leaned against the wall.

"Well, I'm not sure what I can do for you."

"I just needed to talk to you."

"Who are you?"

She flipped her straight blonde hair to the side, away from her face and extended her hand to Joe.

"I'm Jules Green. I just wanted to ask you a couple of questions."

Joe stared at her and raised an eyebrow.

"What kind of questions?"

"About Pine Bluff."

Their voices echoed in the stairwell. Two surgery interns walked between them and exited through the door.

"What about Pine Bluff?"

"Can we go someplace more private to talk?"

"No, not really. I don't really have any place more private. Ask me here. It's okay."

"You moonlight in Pine Bluff, right?"

I cleared it with our Department Chief, Joe thought. She looked like some sort of hospital middle manager to him.

"Yeah, some. But it's all on my own time."

"I know. I'm not here to cause you any trouble."

"Good. Then why do you ask?"

"I'm with KATV. I'm investigating some strange stories from Pine Bluff."

Joe's heart began pounding in his chest.

"What's going on in Pine Bluff?"

"I don't know, not exactly. I thought you could help me."

"How? I don't see how I can help you."

"Well...I know you recently treated a couple of men who died there. They had a pretty wild story, didn't they?"

"How do you know this?" Joe wiped sweat from his brow. Their voices echoed loudly in the stairwell. "You know, come to think of it, I think we do need to talk somewhere else. It's pretty loud in here."

"Fine," Jules said.

Joe turned, opened the door, and led Jules back into the hallway. They walked in front of the elevators and turned to the right down another hallway leading into an adjacent building. Joe looked around to see if anyone was watching. They stopped in a walkway between the two buildings. The ceilings were low and the carpeted floor dulled the sounds. Joe stood next to the windows.

"This is a better place to talk," Joe said quietly.

"I agree."

"Now, tell me again how you know about the cases in Pine Bluff," Joe said.

"I'm sorry. I can't tell you how I know. Let's just say I have a reliable source."

"Great." Joe rolled his eyes.

"Look, Dr. Mason. I've heard some pretty weird stories, and the two men you treated were part of something. There's been more, just not as public."

"Really?"

"Yeah. If you're willing, we can talk more in depth at my office. It's definitely more private there. I can also guarantee you we'll keep your anonymity intact."

"That's somewhat reassuring."

"Look, Dr. Mason. I do this for a living. You're a doctor, I'm an investigator. I'm trying to find out what's going on in Pine Bluff, and you're curious, as a doctor, about what happened to your patients. Am I right?"

"Yeah."

"Then, come down to my office when you get some time, and we can talk more. I can help you, Dr. Mason."

"Okay, I can probably find some time on Thursday afternoon."

"Great. Just come down to the station in the afternoon. I should be there. Or, you could call me," Jules said. She took a business card out of her pocket and wrote on the back. "This is my cell number. If I don't answer, please leave me a message. I promise I return *all* of my calls."

Joe took the card and placed it in his pocket.

Jules turned and walked back towards the elevators. Joe remained in the hallway. After she turned the corner, he took her card back out of his pocket.

Great, he thought, *an investigative reporter.*

Joe's desk at home was a metaphor for his life, stacked with several piles of work to be done. However, underneath the messy appearance was a semblance of order. Joe could find what he needed; it just took some time. He looked for an e-mail that he had printed from a friend from medical school and finally found it under a stack of insurance forms. Joe laughed to himself, such a model of organization.

Brad Yates, whom Joe had met as a freshman medical student and had remained close, was working on a project in his second year of a research fellowship at the National Institutes of Health in Bethesda, Maryland. He was a very bright student who didn't like the deluge of rote memorization that medical school required, but he managed to make good enough grades, despite his disdain.

Joe dialed the phone number for the laboratory where Brad worked.

"Hello, this is Dr. Greene's lab. How can I help you?" the female voice said.

"Yes...this is Dr. Joe Mason. I'm calling from Little Rock, Arkansas. I was wondering if Dr. Brad Yates is in the lab today."

"Yeah, I think he's in the darkroom. Hold on. Let me see if I can find him." Her voice sounded friendly.

After a few minutes, Brad picked up the phone. "Oh, that sounded so official, 'Brad there is a Dr. Mason from Little Rock on the phone for you.' Long time no hear. Are you still able to play any golf?"

"Yeah, a little here and there. I didn't know who was answering the phone, so I thought I'd make it sound like all business."

"Oh, not to worry, that was Jill. She's Dr. Greene's research assistant. And she's definitely hot. If I were Dr.

Greene's wife, I wouldn't be too happy with her working here."

"So, how's life as a lab rat treating you?"

"Pretty good. We've been working on a joint project with the CDC. We're taking samples from sepsis patients whose cultures never grew any bugs and using my DNA tests to see what we can find."

"Is it working?"

"Shit, yeah. I'm surprised myself. It's strange to get such good results."

"Are you still retaining patent rights?"

"Of course, my lawyer says it's mine, all mine. I like the work, you know, the unknown. But I'd also like to be filthy rich as well."

"When you're rich and famous, will you still claim your old buddies who know you can't hold your Tequila down?"

"Oh, that's hitting below the belt, Joe."

"Listen, Brad. I've got a problem I wonder if you could help me with. I had a case where two men came into the ER in Pine Bluff and died from massive pulmonary hemorrhage within twelve hours. I think it was a bad pneumonia, but we could never isolate an organism."

"What did the autopsy show?"

"Well, that's just it. There was no autopsy. The families denied autopsy, but I have ET tubes with hemorrhagic secretions on them. I wondered if you could work your wonders and tell me what killed these men."

"I assume you got full permission from the families to do this."

"Well, ummm. Let's just say that I'm flying solo on this one."

"Yeah, man. I can do it. It shouldn't be a problem," Brad said. "Now you know this test is pretty damn sensitive. You'll get a bunch of bugs come up positive."

"I know, but if anything outside of normal throat bacteria is there, that could be my bug. What's your address?"

After about ten minutes of reminiscing about the past, Joe hung up the phone. He knew that Brad's test could probably tell him what had happened, that they had died of some kind of bacterial pneumonia. However, he had never seen two men die so quickly and violently, particularly in exactly the same way. He packed the bagged tubes and sent them overnight FedEx to Brad.

Joe planned to meet with the reporter in three days. Maybe Brad could tell him something before they met. He remembered what the prisoners told him. If they died of pneumonia, it was unlikely that the guards deliberately killed them, as they said. Joe thought that he would need to talk to someone at the prison, someone who was there, inside the system. He had just the person in mind: his best friend and neighbor from elementary school.

◆　◆　◆

Jimmy Washington had been in trouble of some kind as far back as Joe could remember. In fourth grade, Jimmy was expelled for igniting a cherry bomb underneath the teacher's desk. It was quite hilarious at the time for everyone in the classroom, except, of course, for the teacher. His destructive antics advanced. In sixth grade, he was arrested for vandalizing the school and burning down the school billboard. He went to a 'reform school' for six months after that episode. The school was indeed a learning experience for Jimmy. Instead of reforming, he learned more tricks from more experienced hoodlums. When he returned, his raucous behavior turned more violent, and he started stealing for money.

He became involved in gang-related crime at age fourteen. He was arrested for his first drug-related crime at age sixteen, and he was finally sent to prison for armed robbery and assault after a particularly violent outburst while robbing the local E-Z Mart, which only yielded forty-eight dollars in cash for all the trouble. He was sentenced to serve fourteen years at Cummins Prison, a state prison about ten miles southeast of Pine Bluff. While in prison, Jimmy established himself as one of the most feared prisoners because of his gang connections and his tendency for extreme outbursts of violence. Joe had last visited him about two years earlier, but not since then.

The drive to the prison was uncomfortable; the temperature was supposed to reach ninety-eight degrees. Joe thought that it was a particularly bad time to be at Cummins as an inmate because they would have to work in the fields farming vegetables for the prison. The work was hot and exhausting; Joe had seen at least three prisoners that summer in the emergency room at the hospital in Pine Bluff for heat-related problems.

He parked in the front parking lot and proceeded through the myriad of checkpoints and searches so that he could talk to Jimmy. Security was particularly tight as the prior month violence had broken out after a visitor had somehow smuggled a hunting knife into the prison. Joe sat at the table, as directed, and waited for Jimmy.

"Joe Mason. Holy shit," a deep voice boomed from behind Joe.

Joe turned around to see the tall and muscular frame of his friend. He wore gray prison overalls stained with sweat and dirt from a hard day's labor in the fields. Joe stood up and shook hands with Jimmy.

"Damn, man. You look different since I saw you last. What's it been, two years?"

"Yeah, about that," said Joe. "Sorry I haven't been down in a while, but. . ."

"That's okay, man. I understand. I wouldn't come down here just to hang out with old friends neither. This place is a hellhole. But you know how I see it. If you're gonna be around sons-of-bitches, be the meanest damn son-of-a-bitch and things'll be alright. I'm on top of the world down here."

"I'm sure you're alright. You always have been."

"What's up? Anything new in the world?"

"Yeah. I'm just about finished with all my doctor training."

"That figures. I knew you'd do all right. You always were smart. I'm glad you didn't get caught up in all the shit I got caught up in. So, you oughta be rich by now, huh?"

"Not exactly, I'm up to my eyes in debt from all the loans from school. Maybe I should rob a bank or something." Both Joe and Jimmy laughed.

"Yeah, and if you get caught, we can share a cell together."

"No way, man." Joe laughed. "I'll do Federal time in some country club prison."

"Well, excuse me," Jimmy said, holding his nose in the air.

"Listen Jimmy, I'm down here for more than just a social call. I've got a problem I wonder if you could help me with."

"Hell, man. If you've got a problem and I'm the solution, it must be some deep shit."

"No, not really bad. I just need some information about something I heard was going on down here."

"There's all kind of shit goin' on down here. I guarantee you, if it's happenin' here, I'll know it," Jimmy said proudly.

"That's exactly why I came to you," Joe continued. "I saw a couple of guys in the ER in Pine Bluff who I think were from here. They said they escaped. One guy was tall, maybe six feet three inches with a pretty tall 'fro. The other guy was a shorter, stockier white guy. They both died of pretty bad pneumonia almost as soon as they got to me. One of them said that the guards deliberately killed them. It sounded like they were infected with something."

"Shit, man. Shut up." Jimmy looked around. "Yeah, there's some weird shit goin' on here. But we gotta keep it quiet..." He pulled Joe closer to him as they sat facing each other, "...'bout two weeks back, couple of guys died after being placed in solitary. I heard from a friend that cleans the solitary cells who saw 'em. Said they looked bad...all kinds of open skin sores. He thought their skin just rotted off. Then, 'bout a week ago, ten more took off somewhere else. Official word was they's transferred to a different prison."

"Transferred?" Joe asked.

"Well, one of the guys was runnin' some dope for me. I know people in every other place around, and nobody's seen him. Dude owed me over five hundred bucks, so you know I wanted to find him. Then a coupl'a days ago, twenty more guys from cellblock D shipped out. A Mexican guy I use went with them. His cousin's on cellblock C here. He was told the dude died after transfer. Said it was pneumonia. After all this shit, we've all thought somebody's takin' transfers for something weird. Shit, man, but we don't think much of it. We're all niggers in here." He pulled at his white skin.

"Any guess as to where they're going?"

"No way. Got no idea. And if I don't know, it can't be found out," he said.

"Thanks, Jimmy. Thanks for the info. I'll keep it quiet." Joe stood up. "If you do hear of anything, call me." Joe handed him a piece of paper with his number on it. "You do get to make the occasional phone call, don't you?"

"Hell, man, with my connections, I could call the fucking White House."

After a little more conversation, Joe left. He thought about what Jimmy had said—that so many men had disappeared. He hoped that the DNA tests would help.

- nine -

Joe awoke with a hangover after a late night with a couple of the junior residents. After a large dinner washed down with several beers, they went to the Oyster Bar for some music and more beers. He hated waking up after such a night; he wasn't as accustomed to it as he had been in college, when he would start the Saturday morning with a Bloody Mary or a Screwdriver to take the edge off his hangover. Now past the days of liquor in the morning, he was doomed to suffer the consequences of drinking too much. He swore never to do it again, just as he had done many times before.

The telephone rang loudly. Everything, it seemed, was loud this morning. He reached for the receiver, not to be conversational, but to stop the ringing.

"What the hell are you trying to do to me?" said the voice on the phone. It sounded familiar.

"Who is this?" Joe answered as clearly as he could.

"This is Brad. I think you're trying to kill me."

"What are you talking about?"

"Those tubes you sent me. They're loaded with ugly bugs."

"What is it?" Joe sat upright in bed, paying no attention to the rushing headache.

"You're not going to believe it—it's *Francisella tularensis*."

"What? Are you sure?" Joe asked.

"It had one of the strongest signals possible. There were also some standard throat bugs like we expected."

"You're positive it was tularemia."

"No doubt about it. It scared the shit out of me. That's a Level 4 bug, you know. If anyone finds out I did this in this lab, I'm in deep shit. The secretions were dried so the chances of infection are slim, but it still scares me."

"Both men had only pulmonary symptoms…no big skin problems or swollen lymph nodes. I've heard of pulmonary tularemia, but it's rare. Definitely not from two men at the same time from a prison."

"You're right, Joe. There's some strange shit going on at the prison," Brad said.

"Brad, I shouldn't tell you any more than I already have. I've found out several other things that help put this together. You absolutely should not tell anyone about this."

"If you think I'm telling anyone I brought tularemia into this lab, you're nuts. It's a secret that I'll take to my grave, I assure you."

"Can you send me copies of your tests? I'll need them."

"Joe, you can have the originals. I don't want any part of it."

"Thanks for your help, Brad. Seriously, thanks."

"Next time, let's just have a beer or something, not something like this."

"Don't mention beer to me right now." Joe was queasy.

"I guess it was a late night."

"Bennigan's followed by Oyster Bar."

"Ouch... I'll call you in a couple of weeks to catch up."

Joe hung up the phone, still amazed by the results. Primary pulmonary tularemia was extremely rare, even for Arkansas. He then thought to take what he had to Dr. Sam Bradley. As the Chief of Medicine and Chairman of the Infectious Disease Division, he might know a good explanation for what Joe had found. Joe called Dr. Bradley's office and made an appointment to see him.

◆　◆　◆

Monday afternoon came after an agonizing wait; his appointment time with Dr. Bradley finally arrived. He walked up the flight of stairs to the sixth floor and entered the main office area.

"Hello, Joe," the secretary said.

"I'm here to see Dr. Bradley."

"Of course, take a seat. He's been in the lab all afternoon and is just finishing a meeting with the graduate students. He should be finished anytime. Can I get you some coffee?"

"No thanks. I'll just wait over here."

Joe sat in a vacant chair in a row that lined the far wall opposite Dr. Bradley's office.

After about ten minutes, the door to the office opened; five graduate students filed out with notebooks in hand. They were talking about how to divide the next steps of their project between themselves.

"Come on in, Joe." Dr. Bradley said from behind his desk, which was hidden from Joe's view.

"Hello, Dr. Bradley. I'm sorry to bother you," Joe said as he walked into the office.

"It's never a bother. What's on your mind?"

"I want to tell you about a case that I saw in the ER in Pine Bluff. I need your opinion on what I should do. This is a very awkward situation, so I hope that for now this conversation is completely confidential."

"This sounds interesting. It should go without saying that our conversation will be kept between us."

"I saw a couple of patients in the ER at Pine Bluff when I was moonlighting. They were both escapees from Cummins prison. They both died from what appeared to be massive pulmonary hemorrhage shortly after arriving at the hospital. Chest X-rays on both men showed a diffuse patchy infiltrate. One of the prisoners told me that they were deliberately made ill by some of the guards at the prison."

"Oh my God." Dr. Bradley swallowed hard as he listened further.

"I wouldn't have thought much of it, but being curious I followed up on what I thought would be an obvious autopsy case, but I was told that the families refused permission for the autopsy. It was strange that the two men came into the hospital as John Does, but the families were notified within about two hours. I talked to the pathologist, and he said while it was unusual to be contacted by the families so quickly, there was no obligation to do the autopsy because the men died of what looked like pneumonia. Then, I got the endotracheal tubes, which had dried secretions on them, and sent them to Brad Yates."

"Isn't he at the NIH doing research?"

"Yeah. He has a DNA test that can test for any bacteria. You won't believe what he found."

"By your being here, I take it that it was unusual."

"Absolutely. It was *Francisella tularensis*."

Dr. Bradley swallowed hard again. "Well, that's not uncommon here in Arkansas."

"I know that tularemia isn't uncommon here, but there were no skin lesions and no swollen lymph glands, which I would expect. Both cases were primary pulmonary infection, which is very uncommon. I don't see how the men could get this while in prison."

"I agree it's unusual but certainly not impossible."

"Okay, but I went to see a friend of mine who is at Cummins as an inmate."

"Friends in high places, huh?" Dr. Bradley laughed.

"Yeah," Joe laughed as well. "He was aware of several incidents where prisoners had been taken from the general population. He said many of them died later. Some of them died of pneumonia as well."

"How does he know this?"

"He's very well-connected."

"So let me get this straight." Dr. Bradley leaned back in his chair and took a deep breath. "You think that your prisoners were taken from the general prison population and deliberately infected with tularemia. It seems ridiculous. Why would anyone want to do that?"

"I don't know. That's why I came to you...to see what you thought. You know people. Maybe you can find out what's going on."

Dr. Bradley leaned forward and placed his arms on the desk.

"It does sound like a terrific story, but I'll bet there's a perfectly reasonable explanation. I'll make some calls, quietly, and see what I can find out."

"That's what I was hoping you'd say."

"I'll ask one thing in return. Please keep this between us. I'd hate for this to get out and be misconstrued as something that it's not."

Dr. Bradley stared intently at Joe, which made Joe feel a bit uneasy.

"I don't want any extra attention. That, you can be sure," Joe said as he stood up to leave.

♦ ♦ ♦

Joe parked his car outside the studios of the local ABC network affiliate, KATV; he walked through the large doors and entered the main lobby. It was smaller than he expected, enclosed in glass with a full view of the street outside. The glass muffled the street noise but allowed ample light to fill the space. He approached the receptionist at the counter.

"Hello," the receptionist said in friendly tone.

"Hi. My name is Joe Mason. I was supposed to meet with Jules Green regarding a story."

"I'm sorry, sir. Normally, Ms. Green requires an appointment."

"Yes, ma'am. She's expecting me. I'm a physician at UAMS and I'm afraid my own schedule is tight. Can you see if she's available?"

"Okay, Dr. Mason. Let me see if she's in her office. Please have a seat while I check."

"Thanks," Joe said as he turned to sit in the waiting room chairs.

The secretary called on the phone and after a short conversation arose from her desk. "Ms. Green has some time, but it'll be a few minutes. Please go through the double doors over there to the right. You'll see the other waiting area."

"Thanks," Joe said as he pushed through the doors.

After a wait, he looked up from the magazine to see Jules standing in front of him. A hair clip held back her blonde hair, and Joe noticed her tan legs.

"Dr. Mason. It's good to see you. Sorry for the wait, but I was finishing a phone call."

"That's okay." Joe stood up from the chair.

"Let's go to the conference room," Jules said as she turned to walk.

Joe followed behind her as she made the short walk down the hallway; he wished that the hallway were much longer. She opened the door and pointed for Joe to sit at the table on the side opposite the door. She sat directly across from him and leaned back in the chair crossing her legs.

"Thanks for coming, Dr. Mason."

"Please, call me Joe."

He felt uncomfortable with her calling him doctor. She was about his age.

"Okay, Joe. I'll get right to the point. I think that somebody is deliberately killing prisoners in Pine Bluff, but I don't know why."

"Really?"

"Yeah. My sources are pretty good. I know of at least fourteen deaths in the last month. Your patients, if they're involved, make sixteen. There may be more."

"I've done some checking on my own," Joe said.

"Really?"

"I sent some samples to a friend of mine for testing. Both men in Pine Bluff were infected with a bacteria called

Francisella tularensis, which causes the disease tularemia. They had pneumonia from the disease, which means they inhaled the bacteria. While naturally occurring pulmonary tularemia is possible, it's quite rare. For two men to die within hours of each other with identical exposure history, there's a story as to how they became infected, even if it was naturally occurring. But prisoners shouldn't be involved in any activity to get such an infection. The chances of two men getting naturally infected with airborne tularemia in a prison are probably less than you and I getting struck by lightning right where we sit."

Jules placed her elbows on the table.

"I watched these two guys die in Pine Bluff. Let me tell you, it was awful," Joe added.

She stared out the window over Joe's right shoulder and sighed.

"Who else knows about this, Joe?"

"Just a couple of people, aside from you. I sent the samples to a friend from med school who's doing research at the NIH in Maryland. He did the testing. I also talked to a professor of mine. He's got pretty good political connections. I asked him to check into the stories."

"We need to keep this as quiet as possible, Joe."

"I understand."

"Talk to your friend who did the testing. What was his name again?"

Joe looked at her but said nothing.

"Look, Joe. I'm someone you can trust. I protect my sources. Without trust, I can't get anywhere with what I do."

After an uncomfortable pause, Joe looked back at Jules. "Brad Yates."

Jules wrote the name down in her notebook. "Tell him to keep everything quiet."

"He will. Trust me."

"Who is your professor?"

"Dr. Sam Bradley. He's the Chief at the VA Hospital as well."

"And he'll keep things quiet?"

"Definitely. He thinks there's a good explanation for these cases. He wants to keep it quiet until he can find out for sure. He's okay."

"I've got some more work to do as well, to check some additional things. Can we get together again?"

"Sure."

"How can I get in touch with you, Joe, after I've done some checking?"

"Either my pager or my cell phone are the best." Joe scribbled the numbers on an index card from his pocket. "You can also call the hospital if you need to. They can always find me."

"Great. You have my cell number as well. You can leave a message if you need to, but if it's important, don't just leave a message—find me and talk to me. I'll do the same."

"Sure. That makes sense," Joe said.

"I'll call you in a couple of days to get together."

"Okay, but I'll be on call at the hospital on Tuesday, so be aware of that."

"No problem, Dr. Mason. I'll call you."

Jules stood up from the table and reached across to shake Joe's hand.

"Thanks, Ms. Green. I'm interested in what you can find."

Joe walked around the conference room table towards the door.

"I've got a guy who can find out anything about anything, or anyone. He's the best," Jules said.

"I hope so."

"Thanks, Joe. I'll call you in a couple of days so we can get back together."

Joe walked down the hallway towards the main door. As he walked through the door, he looked back towards Jules, who was watching him walk out.

- ten -

Doctor S reviewed the intelligence reports and knew that he had a big problem—knowledge of the Project existed outside the confines of his direct supervision. The escape of the prisoners had led to outside treatment. The intelligence showed that now the cases were being investigated. This was truly an urgent problem, as big as the previous attacks in airports. Those attacks were bad in terms of potential loss of life, but outside knowledge of the Project threatened its existence, which if scrapped, would cause much greater loss of life.

The knock at the door startled him.

"Sir, you requested to see me." The tall dark-haired man entered to receive orders.

"We need to extend surveillance to top level."

"Who are we to watch?"

"The name is Dr. Joe Mason. He works at the Medical Center in Little Rock. I'll have the secretary give you the exact contact information. He's been under general watch, but now I want to know everything: where he goes, who he is with, what he is saying, what he is eating, when he craps…I mean everything." Doctor S stood from his chair at the desk. "I cannot express just how important this particular case is. I also want this case to be private. All information goes through me and nobody else. Is all of that clear?"

"Crystal clear, sir."

Doctor S stared at the man standing in front of the desk. "Do not screw this one up. This is important."

"We'll do our best, sir."

"For the rest of this week, you and I will meet every morning to go over the results of your surveillance. Is seven a.m. too early?"

"Not at all, sir. See you tomorrow morning." The man turned and left the office.

Doctor S turned away from the door and stared out the window, looking down on the grounds below. There was another knock at the door.

"Doctor…?" the secretary said.

"Yes, Grace?"

"Dr. Henderson is here to see you."

"Great, send him in."

Doctor S thought back to 1961 when he had met Tom during internship. Life was different back then. Medicine was a field overwhelmingly dominated by men; the training was intense by anyone's standard and at times cruel. Those who survived were all changed by it. The work ethic that it molded was pathological, and Tom was a good example. He divorced his first wife after only three years of marriage and one child. He remarried after two years, and after two more children and six more years, his second marriage ended. His third marriage remained intact as he finally learned to cut his work back to sixty hours a week. He couldn't cut back further because of the alimony payments for which he was still responsible.

"Hey, Tom," Doctor S greeted him at the door.

"Hey. I'm here to get that tour you promised. You called me three weeks ago for this work, but I still haven't seen what's actually going on."

"I'm sorry for the delay, but we've been pretty busy."

"So have I, reviewing all of those damn reports you keep sending. I just want to see it all in person."

"You need to see it. That's for sure." Doctor S led him out of the office into the reception area. "You already know Grace."

"We met a few minutes ago."

"Let's go down the main hallway to the lab first." He placed a hand on Tom's back and walked beside him down the wide hallway. "This building was finished in 1952, shortly after the Arsenal was converted to mainly bioweapons production and research. The whole program was completed in about eighteen months between 1951 and 1953. The Arsenal was the largest bioweapon production facility in the world, I'm told, peaking in production between 1955 and 1957."

"I'll bet they don't put that down in the Chamber of Commerce newsletter," Tom laughed.

"Well, you'd be surprised. They don't try to keep it a big mystery, either, because this place brings a lot of money and jobs to the local economy. Even before the Project got here, they were setting up biodefense labs under Homeland Security."

"Yeah, but I've lived here my whole life, and I didn't know any of this was going on down here until you called me."

Doctor S opened the large gray metal door on the right, halfway down the hallway. Through the door, the room was large, with several rows of laboratory benches near the windows and ventilation hoods on the wall near the hallway. The technicians barely noticed the visitors.

"This is one of the main labs. We've got three sections. This is Research. I'll show you the other two, Production and Testing, after this. The whole lab is probably the best vaccine lab in the world."

"Sad statement considering the need for vaccines in the world."

"You're right, but after the lawyers got through with the vaccine companies, there's only three left worldwide. It's incredible."

Tom leaned against the wall, listening.

"Over there against the far wall is the automated protein sequencer. It's based on the work of a professor from California in automating potential vaccine targets. We load the sample into the wells. It's digested enzymatically and spun down in the centrifuge, then the resulting layers are sorted based on molecular size and loaded into these small cassettes." Doctor S handed him a small plastic device with clear depressions on one side and an electronic circuit board on the other.

"It's small," Tom said.

"It is, but let me tell you, it's powerful. I think the professor who invented it will go to Stockholm someday and accept his Nobel Prize. What it does is automate what used to take weeks and months to do. We can sequence every single protein from an organism with this and test for immunological activity. That allows us to go further with only the most promising candidates for the vaccine."

They walked down the side of main laboratory past ventilation hoods on the left side. The low roar of the hoods drowned out the other noise from the lab.

"So, what have you found for this bug? I mean how many candidate antigens have made it through?"

"We've scanned over two thousand genes for this bacteria with this process. After the first round, which took only thirteen days with this process, we ended up with thirty-four candidates."

"Are they done, then, here I mean? Are they done with the genetics and protein work?" Tom asked.

"Mostly for our Project. But since this worked so well, USAMRIID has them working on other bugs to develop vaccine candidates. The last several days they've been working on anthrax."

"Do you think they'll work on more bacteria?"

"Definitely...and viruses. This process is amazing. It can be extended to nearly any microorganism. We hope to have mostly civilian research when we're done here." Doctor S opened the door ahead of them. "Come on down to the next lab. It's the Phase Two area for testing."

The two men walked through the main hallway to the end of the building. After a brief walk outside, they arrived at the next building, which was marked with a large biohazard sign. Beyond the first door was a small reception area with chairs lining the walls and a small glass-enclosed room with a security guard inside. Doctor S passed his name badge in front of the black box near the door. A short beep sounded, and the large metal door unlocked.

"Come through here," Doctor S said as he walked through the door with Tom. "The security from here forward will be tight. It's in place not only for national security reasons but also for biohazard reasons. As you know, this bacteria is a Level Four biohazard."

Tom followed Doctor S through the security checkpoint into a smaller room with two doors in front of them.

"These doors lead to the dressing areas." Doctor S pushed though the door on the right that led them into a locker room.

"Reminds me of my high school gym locker room," Tom said as he laughed.

"All except the smell," Doctor S replied, laughing as well.

"Pick one of the open lockers over there and put on the green scrubs. We're going into Level Two and Three labs, so we have to change."

Once in scrubs, the two men left the locker room and entered a large laboratory. Slightly larger in size than the first lab, the room was surrounded by cages, holding many different animals: rabbits, small rhesus monkeys, and pigs.

"These are the first line subjects for immunology testing. We start mostly with skin testing. On the other side of the wall there we do inhalation work."

Tom looked across the room towards the wall. He noticed a glass enclosure with two technicians working with several rabbits in an enclosed glass cage. Large rubber hoses connected the glass cage to the wall.

"Do those hoses carry the inhalation medium?" Tom asked.

"Yeah, good eye, Tom. We control concentration tightly to see minimum infectious doses and minimum concentration for immune response. We're going around the corner behind that wall to the lab on the other side."

They proceeded through the lab and walked down a short hall into a small control room. Three technicians sat in front of large panels of instruments and computer screens.

"These techs control the experiments throughout the lab. They also monitor the air handlers throughout. If anything triggers, it signals here first." Doctor S leaned over to the technician. "Did you finish with number fourteen?"

"Yes, sir," the man replied. "We're actually completing sixteen now."

"Excellent, you're ahead of schedule."

"Yes, sir."

Doctor S turned to leave the room. "Nice work, guys."

"This is quite a maze through here." Tom noted.

"It seems that way at first, but we have everything divided into zones based on work type and biohazard status. We don't have the Level Four labs here. They're in the outside area. We'll see that later."

"Why aren't they here?"

"The Level Four labs are the end stage testing. For security reasons, they're the tightest. We needed to separate them from this work. This work is fairly straightforward, but the Level Four work is not. It's harder—in many ways."

"I understand."

"Come through here to the Level Three lab. I want to show you this."

They walked into another small room with a glass door.

"Make sure the door closes behind you. We're entering a negative pressure area." Doctor S checked the door behind Tom. "Your ears will likely feel the pressure change."

The air pressure in the room changed, and both men yawned to try to equalize their ears.

"I still hate that part," Doctor S said.

"Oh, it's not so bad," Tom replied.

"Just wait until you do it several times a day. You'll change your tune."

"You're probably right."

Doctor S then pressed a large red button on the wall next to the glass door. After a small beep, the door unlocked. They walked through the door into a broad hallway with a glass wall extending completely down the hall on the right side. Beyond the glass wall, technicians worked in white suits with hoods.

"Okay, so they're completely enclosed?" Tom asked.

"Yes. The suits are completely sealed, including ventilation. Everything's considered infectious here. We won't gown up or go inside. At least not today." Doctor S nudged Tom. He knew that Tom was claustrophobic.

"You aren't going to make me put one of those things on, are you?"

"No. I wouldn't do that to you. Come on, we'll move on. I just wanted you to see the whole place. It'll help you understand what work is being done where. You're here for your brain, not your lab rat skills."

They left the hallway through a door on the left. After passing through another small control room, they entered a glass-enclosed booth.

"I really don't like this part," Doctor S said. "Now, close your eyes. It's going to get windy in here."

Tom closed his eyes tightly as the air inside the chamber rapidly circulated around them. After twenty seconds, it stopped.

"You can open your eyes for a second," Doctor S said. "The air wash is sent through a detector to ensure we haven't carried any contaminants. The second stage is different."

"What do you mean?" Tom asked nervously.

The technician waved from behind the glass to Doctor S.

"Okay, Tom, close your eyes again. And it's going to warm up."

Six bright flashes of light followed, warming their skin.

"Okay, Tom, we're done."

Tom opened his eyes. "What was that?"

"Six pulses of EM radiation, broad frequency, including ultraviolet. The scrubs you're wearing are transparent to UV light. The pulses serve to kill any undetected organisms."

"You're not worried about melanoma?" Tom laughed.

"Hell no, and we're thinking about charging extra for the tanning session," Doctor S laughed as he opened the door in front of them, leading back to the locker room. "Let's get dressed and eat some lunch. I'll drive you to the Level Four lab after lunch. We've set up your office there."

"Inside the Level Four lab?" Tom said as he raised his eyebrow.

"Not inside. I told you. You won't have to put on a spacesuit. I promise. But that's where the high level testing and production are done, so that's where you need to be. You're here for the patients."

"Thank God," Tom said as he dressed.

♦ ♦ ♦

Jules walked out to the parking garage to her car, a red BMW 325i. This was definitely her car.

She opened her cell phone and dialed. After three rings, a strong male voice answered.

"Hello," the voice said gruffly.

"This is Jules."

"Jules, damn glad to hear your voice." The voice softened. "Are you still the most beautiful woman in the world?"

"Are you still the biggest and meanest bastard this side of the Mississippi River?"

He exploded in laughter. "You certainly know how to sweet talk."

"Seriously," Jules said, "I need your help with a job. This one's bigger than I can handle all by myself."

"Jules, if you are admitting to needing help, then I'm all ears."

"I can't talk over the phone. Can I buy you dinner?"

"You can always buy me dinner."

"Meet me at The Villa in, say, two hours. Is that too late for you?"

"No way. I'll be there."

The restaurant wasn't too crowded, subdued in both lighting and ambience. Two couples sat at the table closest to the door, while a single male patron sat in a booth against the far wall reading a newspaper while eating his salad.

Jules sat at the booth on the wall opposite the single man. She ordered a bottle of Merlot and waited for Billy Wood, a friend she had met in Dallas. He was a physically intimidating person at six feet six inches tall and two hundred fifty pounds; he looked more like a football player or a professional wrestler. He was a very effective private investigator, though, and Jules had continued to use him at times ever since he had moved back to Little Rock and she had started her job with KATV.

Billy arrived about five minutes late, which was unusual for him. He motioned to Jules as he walked over to her table.

"I've already ordered a bottle of wine," said Jules brightly.

"Way ahead of me, huh?" He leaned down and kissed her cheek.

"I hope Merlot is okay."

"That's perfect. Why are you buying me dinner? What trouble am I getting myself into?"

"No trouble, Billy." Jules sighed. "I don't always cause you headaches...do I?"

"Jules, your business is always welcome, but I always factor in some recovery time afterwards."

"Well, this job should be fairly simple. I need you to do some background checking for me."

"Who's the lucky person?" asked Billy, as he sipped his wine and leaned back in his chair.

"I had quite an initial meeting with a guy today who has some pretty intriguing stuff. I want to make sure he's not some crackpot. I just want basic stuff."

Billy again sipped his wine. "That sounds pretty straightforward. But knowing you, it'll twist and turn into something bizarre."

Jules laughed. "No way. This guy seems normal. He's a young doctor at the Med Center. The name is Joe Mason. I just don't know much about him. His story makes me a bit nervous, though."

"I'll take care of it. Consider it done. By the way, what's the story, if you don't mind me asking?"

"I'd rather not say right now. I don't want to prejudice you."

"Fair enough." Billy bit into a piece of bread.

"Hey, Billy, how's your mom?"

"Oh, she's doing better. She's still on her own, keeping a big garden, and she still cooks for her baby boy."

Jules laughed. "Yeah, you're such a baby."

"What about you, you sexy thing? Anything hot going on in your life?"

"You know me, not much interesting. I've stopped going out."

"Giving up on men, are you?"

"Not completely. It's just hard to meet someone normal. I don't think there's any normal people left in the world."

"I know what you mean. I can't find a good date either. I'm big, old, fat, and balding…not much of a hot property."

"Oh, come on, you're not *that* old," Jules said with a laugh.

"Thanks, Jules. You're so helpful. Hey, to change the subject a bit, did you get your mom's stuff settled?"

"Yeah, I did. I appreciate your help, Billy…really."

"No problem. That guy was a real asshole."

"Ever since she died, nothing's gone right."

"Well, at least we got her house settled. That guy just needed someone to explain the situation to him."

"Billy, whatever you did, and I don't think I want to know, but whatever you did, it really worked."

"I didn't do anything bad. I just…um…talked to him."

Billy sipped the wine some more as he smiled at Jules.

"Whatever. But thanks, seriously. I'm just glad to have it over and done with. Now, it's just me."

"Well, you know," Billy said as he took Jules's hand, "I'm always here if you need me. You'll always have family as long as I'm around."

"Thanks, Billy. Why weren't you around like a big brother when I was in high school…when I really needed you?" Jules laughed.

Billy laughed as he perused the menu. "Now…you're buying, right?"

"You got it, man. The sky's the limit," Jules said as the waitress approached.

"In that case I'll have the sampler appetizer and the sampler meal, plenty of food for a growing boy."

"I'll have the salad," Jules said as the waitress scribbled the order.

- eleven -

Joe awoke sweating at 5:03 a.m. Sleep was a challenge at times, so he got up from bed, walked into the bathroom, and started the hot water in the shower. He dressed for work and was ready to go by 6:15. He needed to talk to Brad Yates, but he wasn't an early riser, so he was likely to be at home in bed. Joe looked for the phone number, and after a brief search, he finally found it under last month's water bill.

Brad answered the phone with a groggy voice; he was still in bed.

"Hey, sleepy head. This is Dr. Mason."

"Shut up with the doctor shit. Why are you calling me at this hour? I work for the government. Our day does *not* start at seven a.m."

"Damn, grump. I'm just kidding with you. Hey, it's important why I'm calling. I wanted to talk about the specimens I sent you."

"Yeah, what about 'em?"

"We need to keep this between us."

"What do you mean, Joe? Are you in some sort of trouble? Are you getting me in trouble?"

"No trouble. Not yet."

"Oh, that makes me feel much better."

"Just keep it quiet."

"No problem, Joe. I'd keep it quiet anyway because I'm not supposed to be doing any outside testing. What's going on there? What are you into, Joe?"

Joe took a deep breath.

"Oh, I don't know what's going on. I may have stumbled onto something I wasn't supposed to. I just don't want you involved in it."

"You're scaring the shit out of me, man."

"Look, Brad. I can cover my own back…that I promise. I just don't want to have to worry about you too."

The phone line stuttered with static.

"I follow you, man," said Brad. "Take care, Joe."

"Good-bye, Brad," Joe said and hung up the phone.

♦ ♦ ♦

The white van parked outside Joe's apartment blended well into the background of the neighborhood. It was marked with a logo for Mike's Plumbing Company. With all of the small apartment buildings in the neighborhood, a plumber's van was a common sight. Inside the van, two men monitored Joe's life. The smell of old coffee and body odor was thick.

Two days before, the men had placed several microphones inside Joe's small apartment. It hadn't taken them long to search it as well. All conversations inside the apartment and over the phone were monitored. The information coming from Joe's apartment and his life were simply background noise to outside people. It is funny, one man thought, how events that seem so significant to one person are utterly meaningless to others. What mattered, obviously, was context.

The last phone call, however, wasn't meaningless. Through the hours of noise they had collected, the last phone call was a gem. They knew that it would be used to make decisions.

The dark-haired man leaned to the computer and replayed the conversation while a backup recorded to a second computer's hard drive.

"We have excellent sound quality," he said proudly. "But the static is a problem."

"I told you that the dual microphone placement works better. I know what I'm talking about."

"Dude, I never disagreed. I just said that I'd never seen it before. I didn't doubt you," he said.

"Where do you think the static is coming from?"

"Could be anything in there—the cordless phone, the microwave, the wireless network across the street. Anything."

"You don't think it'll be a problem, do you?"

"No, we'll be fine. What time is it?"

"We're out of here in an hour..."

♦ ♦ ♦

The smell made Joe's mouth water. This meal was by far Joe's favorite: a sausage and pepperoni pizza with double cheese. He had already ordered so that it would be ready when Jules arrived. She had called again to let him know that she would be a few minutes late. Joe had finished at about 6:30 p.m. Hospital rounds with Dr. Moon had extended past when they were supposed to end. He had lectured eloquently about the history of medical uses for leeches. Joe laughed at the thought of ordering leeches for a patient.

The restaurant, US Pizza, was what Joe thought any true pizza joint should be. It had out-of-date furnishings, six televisions tuned to sports, waiting staff with attitude, and above all else, cold draft beer. It also helped that it had simply the best thin crust pizza in the world.

Joe had been surprised when Jules called earlier to arrange a meeting. Since their first meeting, he had been looking forward to seeing her again. Jules walked through the double doors and heads turned. She had tried to dress down from work wearing a simple T-shirt tucked tightly into her jeans, but all it did was make her appear more attractive.

She was thin, but with strong body lines, which Joe hadn't noticed when they first met.

"Sorry I'm late, Joe," she said quietly as she approached the table.

Joe stood as she approached and pulled out a chair. "Do you want a beer or something?"

"Beer would be great," she replied with a smile.

Joe motioned to the man at the register.

"I'm so happy to get out of my work clothes. I hate miniskirts and heels. I think television reporters are the last women in the world who continue to dress like that. It sucks."

"Yeah, I hate it when I have to wear skirts and heels," Joe said.

Jules smirked. "Oh, I'll bet you look great in a miniskirt and heels."

"Of course." Joe laughed.

The television showed skateboarding on ESPN2. Jules looked at the screen and laughed.

"Who would possibly look through the listings and say 'Hey, great, skateboarding is on'. I mean really," said Jules.

"I didn't think much of it, but now that you mention it, I can't say that I've ever gone looking for a good skateboarding show."

"Hey, what kind of pizza did you order?" asked Jules.

"A heartburn special…pepperoni and sausage."

"Sounds great."

"Before I forget, I talked to my friend who did the testing for me and told him to keep things quiet. He said not to worry. He'd get into trouble if anyone found out he did the testing anyway."

Jules looked away from the TV towards Joe. "You didn't tell him what you think is going on, did you?"

"Oh, hell no. I'm treating this as a need to know thing. And I don't think anyone needs to know."

"Good. Hey, have you heard anything from Dr. Bradley? Wasn't that his name?"

"Yeah, that's right, and no...I haven't heard anything yet."

"You think he's pretty reliable. I mean he can help get information."

"Yeah, if anyone can find out what's going on, Dr. Bradley can. He knows everyone."

"He sounds like a good contact for me to have—even for the future. I need to meet him at some point."

"You'd like him, Ms Green. He's smart, but pretty down to earth. Just like you."

Jules smiled. "Are you flirting with me, Dr. Mason?"

Joe smiled back. "Did you do any research on your own? Have you been able to find out anything?"

"I still have some people working on it. I also have some good contacts, but I haven't heard anything yet. I'll let you know when I find something out. I was hoping to have something more by today, but I don't."

"You'll let me know when you hear something from your people, right?"

"I will. Maybe something by the end of the week."

"So...if you don't have anything yet, why did you call to meet?" Joe asked.

"I wanted you to know I'm still interested...in the case."

"I see."

"Joe, I get about ten stories a month. Out of that ten, maybe one is interesting. Your story is one of the most interesting."

"I understand," Joe said as he took a sip of beer.

The waitress brought the pizza and set it on the table.

"I'm starving," Jules said as she reached for a plate. "You might not be able to tell from outward appearances, but I love pizza and beer."

"You're my kind of woman," Joe said.

"I hope so, Dr. Mason."

- twelve -

Billy knew that when Jules asked him to check background on somebody, it was always interesting. He had decided to follow Joe for a couple of days and just observe. He knew that the time he spent observing his subjects was the most important. Gathering background information was meaningless without knowing the personality of the subject, which better enabled predictions about behavior. As previously planned, he called Jules to arrange a meeting to review his findings.

He called Jules on her cell phone, but there was no answer, so he left a voicemail message. He never liked leaving messages, because they were traceable, evidence of what a person was doing and when. Billy liked complete anonymity. He was so adamant about this that he had no credit cards and wrote no personal checks. He paid for almost everything in cash or cashier's checks: food, cars, even his house.

Jules finally called him back. They agreed to meet at the television studio at about 3:30. Billy drove down early to walk through the streets of downtown. The hustle of people was comforting—he found anonymity in crowded places. He walked through the double doors and asked the receptionist to call Jules. After calling, she escorted him to the conference room to wait. He poured himself a cup of coffee, powerful coffee, left over from lunch.

"Hey, Billy. I hope you didn't wait long. It's been a nightmare day here. Peter, the news chief, is on the warpath. Nothing's gone right. What did you find out?"

"Well, your Dr. Mason is an interesting subject, as usual."

Jules interrupted. "What do you mean, 'as usual'?"

"Oh, Jules. I'm usually checking on a husband of a pissed off wife or some boring stuff like that. But your people are always something else."

"So you did find some things."

"Well, to start, your Dr. Mason is one smart son-of-a-bitch. His dad skipped out when he was a young boy, and his mom died when he started high school. He petitioned the court, on his own, mind you, to be able to support himself. And he succeeded. He worked at night and on weekends at the local Holiday Inn doing room service delivery and summers doing construction work. He got a full scholarship to the University of Chicago where he studied philosophy and biochemistry. His 1530 on the SAT test helped."

"Holy, cow," said Jules. "What'd you get on your SATs?"

"Not nearly that high."

"Me neither. I don't test well."

"That's what they all say," Billy continued. "After finishing the University of Chicago summa cum laude with dual degrees in biochemistry and philosophy, he went on to medical school at Arkansas. He turned down offers from several other schools because he wanted to go home. He finished medical school number one in his class and is now finishing his residency. I took the liberty to follow him in his daily routine, which is what I do for everyone, but what I found was quite remarkable."

"Oh, Lord. Here comes the punch line."

"We're not the only people interested in Dr. Joe Mason."

"What?" Jules stared at Billy.

"We're not the only people interested in Dr. Mason. He's already under watch by someone."

"You're kidding, right?"

"No way, he has a tail on him at all times. There's a white van parked outside his apartment when he's there. I'm sure they've bugged the place…he might be bugged himself at all times."

Jules slumped down in the conference room chair and stared blankly out the window.

"I told you it was interesting. I don't have a clue as to what it is he's into, but by the looks of things, someone powerful is very interested in Dr. Mason."

"He came to me with an almost unbelievable story."

"Whatever he told you, I'd believe it. Or, I'd believe he's into something big. Did he give you any idea that he thinks he's being watched?"

"Hell no. He's just a guy who's stumbled into a pile of deep shit. Apparently, he doesn't know how deep."

"Well, I'd probably agree with the deep shit part...you know what you need to do?"

"What's that?"

"Take him swimming." Billy grinned.

"What possible good could that do?"

Jules thought about it. It made sense.

- thirteen -

Jules called Joe the following morning. She was excited about the prospect of taking him swimming. She had found him attractive before she knew much about him, but now he seemed even more alluring. She knew that she should ask him in a subtle way, not to arouse suspicion, either from Joe or the people watching and listening.

She considered several possible ways: ask him for a date somehow disguised as a business meeting, or she could invite other people to make it look like a group thing. That always worked in high school. How childish, she thought—how perfect.

Greer's Ferry Lake, a well-traveled lake by people around Central Arkansas, was about an hour's drive from Little Rock. With clear water and many coves tucked between mountains, the lake offered good privacy for boaters to have some water to themselves, and it would be perfect for her purposes. She invited several people from the television station to go out for the afternoon: Jack Preston, a cameraman, Jill, his wife—they were teased about the 'Jack and Jill,' Javier Santoro, a boom operator, Mandy, his wife, Heather Raftery, a makeup artist, and her partner, Teresa Smith.

Heather and Teresa had been together for eleven years. Some people felt uncomfortable around them as they were openly gay. They reasoned that if they were secret about their relationship, people would still talk about them; so they chose not to be secretive. Jules wanted to see how Joe reacted, and Heather had a boat. They usually rented two Waverunners when they arrived.

Jules called Joe through the hospital operator claiming to be Joe's sister, who forgot his pager number. Joe laughed when the operator asked if he would take a call from his sister, Jules.

"Hey, sport," Jules said cheerfully.

"Hey, sis. How's Mom?" Joe retorted.

"She's great. All is well at home. Dad still plays too much golf."

"Alright," Joe said. "You're starting to scare me."

"Sorry for calling you this way, but I didn't have your numbers on me."

"Some investigative reporter you are."

"Joe, that hurts...I do remember names and numbers for my *big* stories."

"Oh, so I'm just a small fry to you."

"That's right," Jules laughed, "...and don't you forget it. Seriously, what's going on with you this weekend? I was going up to Greer's Ferry this weekend with some friends and wanted to know if you could come."

"Sounds like great fun. I have to see a few patients early in the morning, but I can leave by eleven a.m. Is that too late?"

"Hell, no. I don't wake up until then. I'll pick you up at your place at eleven, then."

"Sounds good. I'll e-mail my address. Do I need to bring anything?"

"Nope, just your body and a swimming suit."

She was excited about seeing Joe in a swimming suit. Again, she felt like she was back in high school.

◆　◆　◆

Saturday morning patient rounds passed painfully slowly for Joe. He arrived at the hospital before six a.m. so that he could get his work done and leave, but Dr. Moon decided to make teaching rounds, with no chance of finishing before noon. Joe told the team before rounds started that he had to leave early for an important meeting.

He arrived back at his apartment at ten-thirty, barely enough time for him to change clothes and gather up towels, sunscreen, and some beer before the red BMW pulled up in front of his apartment. Joe was excited when he saw Jules, wearing very short denim cut-off shorts and a bikini top. Joe wished the whole neighborhood could see him get into the car with this beautiful woman.

Jules leaned over the convertible top. "Should we put the top down for the drive?"

"It's up to you. I'm good either way."

Joe quickly put his sunglasses on so he could stare at her without her noticing as much.

"Since you're putting your shades on, we should put the top down."

She leaned into the car and pushed a button. The top lifted away from the windshield and folded automatically behind the rear seat. Joe walked up to the passenger door and tossed his bag into the back seat. As he leaned into the back, he noticed that she, too, was putting on her sunglasses.

"Nice car, Jules," Joe said as he sat in the front seat.

"Thanks. I love it, especially on days like this when I can put the top down and just drive."

"I agree…it's perfect. You're sure I don't need to bring anything special today?"

"No, we've got everything covered. I'm just glad you could come."

"So am I. I was surprised when you asked."

"I had a good time the other night at US Pizza, so I figured we could spend some more time together today."

Joe leaned back in the seat. "Now this is what I had in mind for a perfect day."

Jules smiled.

"Hey," Joe said. "Not to talk business, but did you find out anything on my stuff?"

"Yeah, a few things, but we can talk later."

"Sorry, but I sort of live with my work, you know. It's a curse."

"It's okay, Joe. I'll get a few beers in you and you'll forget all about it."

"Jules Green…you're going to corrupt me."

"Oh, I don't think so, Dr. Mason. I think your corruption started years ago."

"Damn. Does it show?"

"Oh, you forget, I'm a brilliant reporter, keen on observing people."

"Well, yeah, but I can't figure out if you're that deep or if I'm that shallow."

"Give me some credit, Joe."

They both laughed.

"Okay, but I don't know anything about you," Joe said, "except that you're this brilliant investigative reporter."

"Joe…you say that with such a skeptical tone."

"No, not at all." Joe rolled his eyes.

"Well, Joe, my story isn't really very interesting. I was born in Tyler, Texas, and lived there until I graduated from high school."

"Let me guess," Joe interrupted, "you were captain of the cheerleading squad and dated the prom king."

"Not exactly. I was never a cheerleader. I was a player."

"Really?"

"Yeah, I was a jock. Captain of the volleyball team. State Champs my junior year."

"I'm impressed," Joe said as he imagined Jules in tight shorts, spiking a volleyball.

"I then went to college at Tulane."

"You lived in Sin City?"

"Doesn't it show?"

Joe laughed.

"I moved on from there to a small broadcasting job in Lafayette for a couple of years."

"I'll bet that was interesting."

"Yeah...a nice town, but pretty small."

"Did you go from there to Dallas?"

"Yeah, I went to WFAA, which is where I got into investigative reporting. I worked with a guy there who taught me how to do good investigative work."

"How long were you in Dallas?"

"Just over four years. I got a call from Peter, the manager here in Little Rock. They were looking for someone to head up their new investigative reporting department. He offered, so I came. I love it here."

"You think you'll stay here a while?"

"As long as they'll have me. I feel like I'm home. I've worked hard to get here."

"I can't wait until I can settle into a steady job," Joe said.

"You docs are in training a long time, huh?"

"Yeah, I'm twenty-eight years old and I've still never had a real job. I've been in school or in residency since I was five years old."

"That kinda sucks."

"It does, but I'm nearly done."

"Where do you think you'll end up?"

"I don't know. I've got some offers in several places. I think I may head back north some, to get a cooler climate."

"You're missing the Chicago winters?"

"No, not that far north. Chicago winters suck. I'm just looking for something in between a Chicago winter and an Arkansas summer."

"Sounds good," Jules said and then sipped from her water.

The sun worked halfway to vertical in the sky and warmed Jules and Joe as they drove. As they approached the boat ramp, Joe saw a long line of boats; it was going to be a busy day on the lake. Jules pulled her car up next to one of the boats and yelled to the brunette woman sitting in it.

"Excuse me, miss. Do you have any idea how gorgeous you are?"

Joe stared at Jules in dismay.

The woman on the boat laughed. "Careful, Jules. Heather will get jealous and go after your strapping man in the car there."

"I'm not too worried about that," Jules said. "She won't be too interested in a man. We're gonna park and get some sandwiches. Do you want us to get ya'll something?"

"No, thanks. We're good." She looked down again, "Hey, Jules."

"Yeah?"

"You couldn't find a shirt this morning or are you trying to impress *me*?"

Jules blushed and sped away towards the parking lot.

"I take it she likes women," Joe said.

"Oh, yeah. Very, very gay. But very, very nice. That was Teresa. She and Heather own the boat. They've been together a long time. That doesn't bother you, does it, Joe?"

"Hell, yes. Only I'm supposed to make comments about your cleavage."

Jules blushed again.

◆   ◆   ◆

The sun was high when the group finally got underway. Javier and Mandy rode a Waverunner out of the dock area following the boat. They all sped up when they got to open water. Heather piloted the ski boat to her favorite cove, about a fifteen-minute boat ride away.

Jules drove another Waverunner and Joe held on to her waist as they sped off to the open water into the next cove, which was devoid of other boats. It wasn't conducive to skiing because it was too narrow. He noticed that the hillside that encircled the cove had steep sides. As he admired the cliffs, Jules turned the handlebars violently, tossing both of them into the water.

Stunned, Joe swam to the surface. "What the hell was that for? Damn woman drivers. And ya'll wonder why we complain."

"Ha, ha, ha, Joe."

Jules swam towards the Waverunner and caught it.

Joe swam to the opposite side and around the back towards Jules.

"Can I ask a favor of you, Joe?"

"Sure, Jules."

"Take off your pants."

Joe laughed. "You first."

"No, Joe. I'm serious. I need you to take off your swimsuit and drop it to the bottom." She lifted up the seat and pulled out a new swimsuit. "You can put this one on instead."

"You don't like my swimsuit?"

"No, I don't, and I'll explain why in a minute. Just take off your pants and drop them to the bottom."

Joe stared intently at Jules waiting for the punch line to her joke. Her facial expression didn't change. Begrudgingly, he took off his swimsuit in the water as she handed him the new one.

"I'll explain, I promise," she said.

Joe's arousal at the request when it was made changed to complete confusion. Once he had successfully changed suits,

Jules pulled herself onto the Waverunner and reached her hand down to Joe.

Joe looked up at her and took her hand. "Okay, now you take your top off."

Jules smiled. "Maybe later."

She drove out to the open water of the lake and stopped.

"Now, what? Oh mysterious one."

Jules dove into the water and Joe followed. They both swam back to the Waverunner and held onto the side.

"Now that we can be alone. I need to tell you a few things, Joe."

"Uh-oh. Don't tell me you're gay and you got me naked for nothing."

"I'm not gay, and I got you naked for good reasons," Jules said. "You were bugged."

Joe's jaw dropped open. "Say that again."

"You're under advanced surveillance. This was the only way I knew to be able to tell you without arousing suspicion. They'll think you just got lucky."

"I'm under surveillance? How do you know that?"

"I had you under surveillance."

"You were watching me. What the hell for?"

"All I asked for was a background check—it's routine in our business, please understand. My detective decided to follow you for a while, you know, to see what your daily routine is like. That's when he saw that you were already being watched. Whatever it is that you've seen, somebody important is very concerned."

"Damn." He stared at the water. "So, this entire trip was just a setup to warn me about this."

"Well, no. Not totally. It was still a good reason to get you naked."

He leaned over and kissed her.

"Thanks for keeping me out of trouble," he said quietly.

"Not at all, Dr. Mason. I assure you...it was my pleasure."

- fourteen -

Doctor S stared silently out the window. The recent attacks on the airports had been contained successfully through a great deal of planning and proper execution of contingency plans. This was critically important; the Project must be kept secret, and the doctor in Little Rock was close to opening the door to speculation wide open. It was bad enough that the doctor had a fractured knowledge of it, he thought, but it was intolerable to involve an investigative reporter.

After reviewing the latest transcripts from the surveillance, Doctor S believed that the reporter didn't have any verifiable evidence other than statements from a young doctor. The only tangible evidence was in Bethesda, Maryland, where the young doctor had sent specimens to a friend for testing. Doctor S hated making these decisions, but he knew it was the only way to guarantee ongoing secrecy for

The Project. The doctor in Maryland had to be eliminated, as well as all evidence of the testing he had done.

He notified the CIA team of his decision, and that was the last he would hear of it. He knew that from that point on, the young man's fate was certain. He remembered from his years of military experience that sometimes killing was necessary, but it was still no easier to accept.

Doctor S signed the order and sent it electronically to the stranger whose job it was to carry it out. He sat back in his chair and stared at the ceiling. With each passing day, he felt the weight of his job more intensely than the day before, torn between his responsibility to protect the masses and his unavoidable responsibility to keep all outside knowledge of The Project at bay. The door to his office opened slowly and a woman's face peered around.

"Are you busy, sir? May I talk with you?"

"It's okay. I was just catching up on some computer work."

"I need to talk about your schedule for next week. There will be some changes."

Doctor S leaned back in his chair, thrust back to the daily routine of his administrative job and its necessities. It was comforting to some degree to immerse himself in the routine that shielded him from contemplating the larger picture.

♦ ♦ ♦

Joe awoke the following morning with an excitement he hadn't felt in a long time. The anticipation of what the day might bring was energizing. He had been with Jules all day at the lake. They returned to Little Rock in the early evening, followed by dinner at Doe's Eat Place, an unpolished gem in the world of local cuisine. They walked downtown for a while and ended the night listening to The Cate Brothers, a jazz band, at Juanita's. Several drinks later, memory faded a bit.

He rolled over in bed and saw golden blonde hair covering most of the other pillow. Joe gently got out of bed so he wouldn't disturb her. He went into the bathroom and splashed cool water on his face and stared into the mirror. His hair was a sight, flat on one side and sticking straight out on the other.

"Nice hair," a gentle voice said from behind him.

She placed her hand on the small of his back and moved close behind him.

"I'm well-known for my morning hair at the hospital when I've been on call. It's the source of many jokes." He turned to face Jules and placed his hands around her waist. "Aside from a small hangover, this is easily the best morning of my life."

"I agree."

"You'll have to show me the way around your kitchen so I can make breakfast. My pancakes are killer."

Jules laughed. "If you can cook, I'm going right back to bed because I know I'm dreaming."

"You don't have to go back to bed, and I'm a great cook." Joe pinched her.

◆　◆　◆

The knock at the door startled Brad Yates. He stumbled out of bed and walked into his den and then looked through the peephole in the door. A dark-haired man in a gray uniform stood outside holding a small box.

"Can I help you?" he said loudly.

"I'm sorry to disturb you, sir, but we've had a high-pressure surge through the natural gas lines and I have to check your stove to make sure there's no leakage. We've had several small leaks. It's very important."

"Hold on a minute," Brad said in a disgusted voice, unlatching the lock and opening the door. "The kitchen is through there, towards the back."

The man in gray walked into the den.

"I haven't smelled any gas, man," Brad said with a yawn.

"Some of the leaks have been small, but they're still dangerous. Is it through there?"

Brad walked ahead of the man, leading him into the kitchen. As he passed through the hall, the man in gray pulled him violently to the ground. He hit him in his nose, immediately drawing blood. Stunned, Brad tried to fight back, but was struck again in the nose. The man in gray slipped a wire around Brad's neck and tightened it.

The man in gray continued to hold pressure for about a minute after the struggle ended to ensure that the target was dead. It was remarkably clean; only a small line of blood oozed from the obviously broken nose. He was satisfied with the work.

He found the computer in the bedroom, sat at the keyboard and inserted a mobile drive into the USB port of the computer.

The display read, "Okay for advanced reformat: hit {ENTER}."

The man in gray tapped the enter key and then waited while the hard drive was reformatted and scrambled. The scrambling software ensured that no data recovery was possible from the drive. Afterwards, he unplugged the power cord from behind and connected the cord from the box he brought to the power input of the computer. Once it was connected, he pushed the button on the box. A loud pop echoed throughout the room as the electrical discharge disabled all the circuitry connected to the power supply, effectively destroying the computer. A strong smell of electrical smoke filled the air. He pushed the computer onto the floor, then pulled out drawers, spilling their contents onto the floor, and took clothes out of the closet and threw them around the apartment. Using his knife, he cut the cushions on the couch and chair, spreading the polyester filling throughout the room.

He took the target's wallet and watch and left through the front door. He purposely left the front door slightly open so that it wouldn't be too long until the scene was discovered.

♦ ♦ ♦

Monday morning wasn't too bad, as Joe's life had changed dramatically over the previous three days. Jules provided a spark that he hadn't felt in a long time. The car ride to work was especially enjoyable; he kept the radio off listening only to the quiet hum of the tires on the roadway. The stresses of his job were soon to be unleashed, but this moment was peaceful. Thoughts of spending further time with Jules made the ride that much more pleasant. However, thoughts of being watched all the time bothered him. The solitude of the car seemed suddenly suspect.

He arrived at the parking lot just before seven a.m., as it filled quickly with other resident physicians. Once inside the building, he checked at the office to see what new consults awaited him so that he could plan his day. He took the elevator to the sixth floor and walked to the Medicine office to get a cup of coffee. As he entered the office, Dr. Bradley placed a folder on the secretary's desk.

"Good morning, Joe. I trust you had a pleasant weekend," Dr. Bradley said.

"It was great. I spent some time in the sun at the lake with a friend. It was hard to return to work." Joe poured the black coffee into a Styrofoam cup. "Can I pour you some, sir?"

"No, thanks. I've already had my two cups this morning."

"Only two, I'll be well past that here shortly. One thing medical school and residency have done is fuel my coffee addiction."

"I still remember," Dr. Bradley laughed. "Hey, Joe, by the way, I did some checking into what you asked. Do you think you could come by later in the afternoon to discuss it? I would now, but I have a department chair meeting that I'm five minutes late for."

"Yeah, sure. That'd be great. What time?"

Dr. Bradley reached across the secretary's desk to grab the schedule. "How about 3:30?"

"I'll be here. Thanks."

Joe turned and left the office. He knew that he would have to leave teaching rounds early, and what better reason to leave rounds with Dr. Moon than a meeting with Dr. Moon's boss? Even more important maybe, Dr. Bradley could enlighten him on what was happening.

Joe opened the door to the Infectious Disease office. The weekend doctor had left a list: fourteen follow-up patients and two new consults—not too bad of a morning. He wondered what Dr. Bradley had found.

♦ ♦ ♦

Jules arrived at the studio at about ten a.m., an hour earlier than her normal routine, to finish some copy work on a couple of slow stories that remained. She also thought to have Billy Wood check on Joe's friend in Maryland who had done the testing, to be sure that he was solid. In her experience, the most common leaks in big stories came from the fringes, from the least expected people. As far as Jules knew, he and Dr. Sam Bradley were the only other people that had knowledge of Joe's story.

She entered the newsroom, already bustling with activity, as the noon show set preparations were ongoing. The cameramen had the number three camera nearly totally disassembled, or so it appeared.

"Trouble with your unit, *boys*?" Jules said jokingly as she passed the men.

"No problems at all. Everything's in perfect working order," he replied. "Why do you ask?"

"Oh, no reason."

"Just one more strip of duct tape and we'll have everything in shipshape."

"There's nothing in the world that can't be fixed with duct tape, eh guys?"

"You got it."

The sweet smell of coffee coming from the conference room touched Jules's nose. She didn't restrict her intake of coffee; many times she drank coffee to help control her appetite. A reality of her job was that no one was allowed to be overweight.

She walked over to her desk and thumbed through the papers until she found Billy's phone number.

"Hello. This is Billy."

"Billy, I have another fun-filled job for you."

"Oh, shit. Jules, I don't know if I can take anymore of your 'fun-filled' jobs."

"Oh come on, Billy," Jules said. "I'm the only person who gives you interesting work, right?"

"You've got that right, babe. Seriously, I'd be happy to help. What do you have?"

"This job will involve some travel—to Maryland."

"Why do you want to bother someone all the way up in Maryland? What could they have possibly done to you?"

"This is a close friend of Dr. Mason. I just need you to check his phones and stuff. Make sure the same people who are watching Joe aren't watching him, too."

"There's no telling what's going on with this group. Do you have much contact information for me?"

"No, just a phone number."

"That'll do just fine. I can find out the rest. Now, just to get this straight, all you want me to do is check for other spooks watching this guy, right?"

"That's right. Thanks, Billy."

"No problem, Jules. Glad to do it."

Billy took a deep breath. Jobs from Jules Green always seemed to involve surprises.

- fifteen -

Joe arrived at Dr. Bradley's office about ten minutes early, ten fewer minutes he had to listen to Dr. Moon. The highly relevant rounding topic concerned the historical importance of tuberculosis within Napoleon's armies. The topic, while mildly interesting was of no help in preparing for practicing medicine. He walked into the office and sat in one of the chairs in front of the secretary.

"Hey, Joe. Dr. Bradley is just finishing in the lab. He'll be up here shortly," the secretary said.

"Mildred, when are you going on that Alaskan cruise?"

"Oh, I have thirteen months until retirement. After that, there's no telling where I'll be going. I assure you, I will *not* be spending my summers in Arkansas."

Mildred Sears had been with the VA system for almost twenty-nine years. She was experienced at maneuvering within the governmental bureaucracy. She had seen five presidential administrations in her Federal tenure since starting as a secretary in the Medicine office. She was a stable fixture within the office, serving as secretary for six different chairmen of medicine.

Dr. Bradley walked through the door with a scowl on his face. Obviously all wasn't well in the lab.

"If that no good lazy son-of-a-bitch grad student doesn't have the revisions for this paper by tomorrow morning, I want you to kill him," Dr. Bradley said as he threw the notebook onto the desk.

"Consider him killed, sir." Mildred laughed, nodding her head up and down.

"Come on in, Joe. I'm sorry for the display. As you know, I can't stand lazy people with excuses."

"Me neither, sir. Let's kill all the sons-of-bitches," Joe said.

"That's the spirit. I feel better already."

Dr. Bradley walked into his office and sat down. He leaned back and rubbed his eyes.

Joe sat at the chair opposite the desk and felt awkward sitting in front of an angry Dr. Bradley, even though the anger wasn't aimed at him.

"You said you were able to find out some information for me?"

"Yeah, I did." He reached behind the desk and pulled out a two-page report and handed it to Joe.

Joe read the report with an Arkansas Department of Health logo at the top: a letter to Dr. Bradley regarding an inquiry into scattered outbreaks of pneumonia at the prison in Pine Bluff. It was addressed as confidential, and it outlined twelve known cases of lethal pneumonia at the prison, all confirmed cases of Legionnaire's disease, caused by the bacteria *Legionella pneumophila*. Joe knew that infections with this bacterium were typically linked to infected water reservoirs, like water tanks or air-conditioning condensation units.

"Wow! Is there a known source for the bugs?" Joe asked.

"They haven't yet been unable to find the source. You can imagine the problems they'd have if this were public knowledge. They're doing all they can to isolate the cause. They've moved all the prisoners from the wing that's suspected as the source of the infections, so there's little ongoing risk. But this is obviously a dangerous situation. I suppose the prisoners, such as your friend there, are suspicious of a conspiracy, as several have died and a bunch of others have been moved."

"How did you find out about this?"

"I asked...discreetly. It helps to have worked directly with these people at some point in the past. They're quite competent at public health safety, even of prisoners." Dr. Bradley leaned back in his chair.

Joe thought about the implications. Why did the secretions on the tube he sent to Brad test positive for tularemia? Why did these men die of massive pulmonary hemorrhage, which is very uncommon for *Legionella*?

"Thanks for checking into this matter for me."

"That's no problem. I hope this helps you," Dr. Bradley said as he stood up from his desk.

Joe stood up as well and reached across the desk to shake hands with Dr. Bradley. He turned and left the office but felt somewhat uneasy about the simplicity of the explanation. Brad Yates needs to know about this, Joe thought. Brad would know what to do.

♦ ♦ ♦

Of all the things that his job enabled him to do, Billy loved flying the best. He loved observing people, trying to piece together life stories from small bits of information. Airplanes offered ample sustenance for him to feed on.

The couple sitting two rows in front of him, he thought, are obviously at the top of the scale—visibly in love, smiling with direct eye contact when they spoke to each other. Billy imagined that they were recently married and traveling to a tropical island for their honeymoon.

The man sitting across the aisle was at the opposite end, obviously despondent, his gaze directed downward. He was young and handsome, yet he paid absolutely no attention to the attractive woman seated next to him. He made no attempts to converse with her or socialize. Billy imagined that he had made last-minute reservations to visit a sick relative who was alone in a distant city.

The other people on the flight were within the middle of the emotional spectrum, carrying on the routine of their daily lives. Around Billy was a businesswoman in a smart dark suit tapping away on her laptop computer, two young children and their mother, who was attending to their wants and needs while seemingly ignoring her own, and an older couple seated comfortably and quietly next to each other. The man's hand gently grasped her knee as her hand rested on his. Throughout the flight, the couple never spoke. Apparently, they were so accustomed to one another that conversation wasn't needed.

The flight to Baltimore/Washington Airport was bumpy but otherwise fine. After gathering his bags, Billy rented a car for the short drive towards Washington, DC. The phone number that Jules had given him was for Brad Yates, apparently a friend of Dr. Mason. By typing the phone number into the Google search engine, Billy found the address for the number, which took him to the outskirts of Washington. He was surprised that it had become increasingly difficult to distinguish Baltimore from Washington. The area had grown since he was last here ten years earlier, and the thirty-mile space between the cities was full of housing subdivisions and strip malls.

He arrived at the address and drove up to the apartment building, a repeating theme of four-unit buildings, monotonous across the complex. The numbering scheme was somewhat erratic, but finally Billy located building number twenty-two. Apartment 223 belonged to Brad Yates. Billy knew little about Dr. Yates, just that he was a friend of Dr. Mason in Little Rock and that he was some kind of researcher at the National Institutes of Health.

As he approached the building, the street was empty and the entire building was dark. In the middle of the building, protected from the weather, a stairway led to the second floor apartments. With the sun setting, darkness surrounded the building, making visibility near the stairs poor, but Billy spotted something dangling from the railing. It looked like a party streamer. He circled the building once more to make sure that no surveillance vehicles were obvious, then parked around the side of the building.

As he approached, he saw that the streamer was yellow and blocked the stairway, preventing anyone from going up the stairs. When he got to the stairs, he read the black writing on the yellow banner: "POLICE LINE – DO NOT CROSS".

"Oh, shit," he muttered under his breath. "Jules, you've done it again."

He looked around to see if anyone was watching, then lifted the banner and walked up the stairs to the door. The yellow tape crisscrossed the doorway, and a large white sign on the door read "Crime Scene. Do Not Enter". Red tape connected the door to the doorframe and read "Sealed Evidence".

Billy left quickly knowing that something very bad had happened to Dr. Yates. Billy thought about whether he had any contacts within the DC Police Department. Unfortunately, he had none. He pulled off the road at a nearby convenience store to use the phone to call Jules.

"I've got some bad news for you, Jules," said Billy quietly.

"Damn it, Billy. For once, why can't you find *nothing* interesting?"

"It's your fault for getting involved in these sordid affairs."

"Yeah, yeah, yeah. What did you find?"

"I can safely say that I don't know. I need your help."

"You're the investigator. What am I supposed to do?"

"I just left young Dr. Yates's apartment building. It was completely taped off with crime scene tape. The apartment itself was sealed with evidence tape."

"Jesus."

"Jules, I wanted to see if you could search the news database to see if his name comes up. I don't know anybody up here to check the story."

"Sure. Hold the line a minute while I go to my office computer."

After a couple of minutes, Jules picked up the phone in her office. Billy heard computer keystrokes and mouse clicking as Jules searched.

"Damn it again," Jules said loudly. "They killed him."

"What did you say?"

"From the City Section of the *Washington Post*—'Bradley Yates, MD, a researcher for the National Institutes for Health, was found dead in his apartment earlier today. Police reports declare that he was the victim of robbery and murder. His is the 79th homicide for the year.'"

"Well, I told you this was all bad news. I don't know what your Dr. Mason is into, but it seems to be a pile of shit about neck deep. You need to get him protected."

"Thanks, Billy. I appreciate you sticking your neck out for me."

"I'm glad to do it. I just don't want you to get hurt. It sounds like this is gonna get bad for Dr. Mason, and maybe for you if you're not careful."

"Thanks. I hear you. I'll take care from here."

"I know you're tough Jules, but this time, I think, is different. Watch your back."

- sixteen -

Joe sat at the nurse's station with a chart and pretended to review it. He knew that if he acted busy, fewer people would bother him. He leaned over and lifted the phone to call Brad Yates at home. The phone rang about ten times before Joe hung up. He then dialed the lab where Brad worked; curious, he thought, for Brad to be at work so early in the morning.

"Dr. Greene's lab," the technician answered.

"This is Dr. Joe Mason from Little Rock. Can I speak to Dr. Yates, please?"

After a brief pause, "Um...I'm sorry, sir, but Dr. Yates will not be coming back to work."

"What?"

"I'm sorry, sir, but I can't say more than that."

The technician hung up the phone.

Something is very wrong, Joe thought. Brad was a bit cavalier in his attitude towards life but not his work. He was nearly fanatical in the lab, and if he no longer worked in the lab, something was wrong.

Joe called the lab number back and spoke again to the technician. He was more forceful.

"I'm a close friend of Dr. Yates, and I need to discuss something very important with him. I need to know how to reach him."

The technician was slow in response.

"Dr. Mason, you'll have to call the police department to find out about Dr. Yates. I hate to tell you this over the phone, but Dr. Yates was murdered yesterday in his apartment."

Joe was silent.

"Dr. Mason, I'm sorry but I need to get back to work. I encourage you to call the police department to get the full story. Good-bye."

Joe continued to hold the phone to his ear. He couldn't imagine what Brad would ever do to get himself killed. Joe's only thought was to call Jules.

His pager beeped loudly, and he flinched, startled at the sound. It was Jules at the studio—perfect. He dialed the number quickly.

"Jules Green, please. This is Dr. Joe Mason. I'm returning a page from her."

"Hold the line and I'll get her."

The secretary transferred the call to the newsroom.

"This is Jules."

"Jules, this is Joe. You're not going to believe what's happened."

Joe spoke so quickly Jules barely understood him.

"Let me guess. Brad Yates was murdered," Jules said.

"Oh, man…how did you know that?"

"I sent my investigator to see if he was being watched, like you are. I knew that since your conversations were being monitored, they'd know he was working with you. Billy, my investigator, just called me with the news."

Joe was silent again.

"Joe, this is very important. You must listen to me carefully," Jules said. "Leave the hospital and come to the studio, right now…you're in danger. If these people are willing to kill Brad, they'll kill you too. I've spoken to our news chief, who's agreed to help us until we can sort things out. We need protection."

"Jules, I don't know if all of this is related. I spoke with Dr. Bradley earlier. He checked on the prisoner's story for me. It's not some big conspiracy. It's just an outbreak of Legionnaire's Disease in the prisons. He showed me a note from the Health Department that outlined their investigation. They were keeping it quiet until they knew they'd contained the source."

"Didn't Brad tell you it was tularemia, not Legionnaire's disease?" Jules asked.

"Yeah, that's why I was calling him—to see what he had to say about this."

"Joe…is it possible that Dr. Bradley's not being honest with you?" Jules spoke more softly.

Dr. Bradley walked briskly around the corner onto the hospital ward. He walked up to Joe and stood at the counter in front of him. Joe motioned to him with a finger, letting him know that he was almost finished with his phone call.

Joe's voice changed. "Okay, then. Well you make sure to take really good care of yourself. I'll talk to you real soon." Joe spoke loudly as Dr. Bradley stood in front of him, waiting.

"Joe, what's wrong?" her voice quivered. "He's there, isn't he? Joe, don't trust him!"

"Okay, then," Joe said cheerfully. "Don't forget, I'll meet you at two o'clock."

"You damn well better meet me at two. Right here in the station...don't go anywhere with him. Run away if you have to."

"Okay, bye now." Joe hung up the phone and stood up facing Dr. Bradley and trying to remain calm. "Hey, what's going on? Do you need me?"

"Yeah, Joe. I do need to talk with you. I found out some more information that might be helpful to you. Let's go to my office."

He motioned to Joe to come around the nurse's station and go with him.

Joe felt like running, but something about Dr. Bradley made him still feel like he could trust him. He walked slowly around the counter in front of Dr. Bradley down the hall towards the office.

Mildred sat at her desk, typing on the computer.

"Hey, Joe," Mildred said cheerfully. "Do you want some coffee? I just made a fresh batch."

"Yes, ma'am, that would be great."

"Just bring it in to us, Mildred. We'll be in my office."

Dr. Bradley sounded calm.

Joe walked into the office and sat in the chair. Dr. Bradley followed and left the office door open, which made Joe feel more comfortable.

Jules is overreacting, he thought. Dr. Bradley had nothing to do with Brad's death.

"Hold on a second, Joe." He picked up his phone and dialed. "I'm back in my office, so anytime you want to come up, I'll be here." He then hung up the phone. "Sorry, Joe, but the lab techs are coming up shortly."

Mildred entered and handed Joe a cup of coffee. "Do ya'll need anything else?"

"No thanks, Mildred." Dr. Bradley said. "Oh, Mildred, by the way, when the technicians get up here, just send them in."

"No problem," she said as she left the office.

"Joe, I'm glad I found you. I need to share some new information with you about the pneumonia cases at the prison." He leaned back in his chair and put his arms behind his head. "I'm afraid I haven't been as forthcoming with all of the information as I should have been."

Joe's heart sank in his chest. The technicians stood at the door.

"Come in," Dr. Bradley said.

Two large men in suits came through the door and sat down in the chairs behind Joe. They closed the door as they entered. Joe's heart sank even lower in his chest as the hairs on the back of his neck stood. His stomach churned with a wave of nausea.

"I'm sorry, Joe, but I guess you know why these men are here."

"Yes, I think I do."

"Joe, you're a bright kid, and I need an opinion." He took a deep breath. "I have a very tough job at times. I have to make decisions everyday that affect people's lives in ways you cannot possibly comprehend. You're in a position to make our lives much more complicated...more complicated than they already are. What should I do with you?"

Dr. Bradley leaned forward and folded his arms on his desk and stared intently at Joe.

"I don't know, sir. I'm afraid I don't have enough information to help you. I don't know much at all." Joe's voice trembled.

"You're damn right you don't," Dr. Bradley said. "You have no idea what you're in the middle of."

"Well, sir," Joe said as he leaned forward in his chair. "I'd love to help you with your...situation...as you call it. Why don't you tell me more about it so I can help you?"

"Well, Joe. Let me pose a hypothetical to you."

"Before you start, sir...can these men please leave? They're making me very uncomfortable."

"No, Joe, they stay. You've placed us in a position that's difficult to resolve. These men may be needed to help resolve our problems."

Joe recognized the threat. The nausea returned.

"Joe, what would you do if you had knowledge of a plan hatched by fanatics to kill many American people? And you knew their plans would be successful if you didn't intervene. Also, the only way you could possibly intervene involved sacrificing a few people to save many."

"I don't know what you're talking about, sir," Joe said.

"Remember D-Day, Joe, in World War Two? Hundreds of American men died on the beaches of Normandy. Their deaths were the result of orders from their own commanding officers to storm that beach. The generals knew that many men would die. Did that make their orders immoral?"

Joe stared at the floor.

"Those orders, Joe, saved lives—thousands of lives, perhaps millions. History is marked by countless similar examples. A few die to save many."

"I see what you're saying, sir, but I don't see how that relates to my situation."

Joe peered at Dr. Bradley, trying to read his emotions.

"Joe, what I'm going to tell you is top secret. The reason I'm telling you this is because I want to save your life...Joe, we're at war. Right now, we're at war. It's a secret war, but just as deadly as any in the past. It's remained a secret because we've done everything in our power to keep it that way. It hasn't been easy. But absolutely necessary."

Joe leaned back in his chair. He could hear the breathing of the men behind him.

"Joe, the prisoners you treated died of massive pulmonary tularemia. Dr. Yates was right about that. There was nothing you could've done to prevent their death. There was nothing anyone could've done once they were infected."

"Bullshit!" Joe said. "We can treat tularemia. Those men died miserably. And you're telling me that there was nothing anyone could've done? Well, bullshit!"

"I assure you, once those men were infected, they were dead men. That's my point. Listen to what I'm saying. They were infected with a genetically re-engineered strain of tularemia. This bug is simply the worst bacteria that has existed on this planet—ever. It was created by an Iraqi scientist, Dr. Ali Abul-Aziz, who ironically trained here in the States at Cal-Tech, where he did some of the most revolutionary work ever done in genetic engineering of bacteria. He went back to Iraq to complete his mandatory military service. While there, he continued his bacterial work, but in the area of biological weapons development. His work there was just as revolutionary. He disappeared shortly before the invasion of Iraq."

Joe swallowed hard as he listened.

"We discovered the fruits of his labor with considerable expense—both in money and in lives. At least four men died getting us our first information. We were able to steal some of his samples in transit from his lab outside of Baghdad. What we found was incredible—a strain of tularemia with a thick capsule for environmental stability. This tularemia could survive for days in direct sunlight without water and still be infectious. He also inserted several genes for antibiotic resistance. In short, he created the apocalypse bug, and they intended to use it. They had plans for a two-stage attack, both on Israel and the United States. We were able to avoid those attacks because we successfully destroyed all of Dr Aziz's lab facilities. Unfortunately, several smaller batches escaped the attack, and they are now in the hands of terrorists who are well-funded and ready to attack the United States directly. We've had four small attacks on targets within the United States in the last three months. We've been able to contain them to a point, but we have had loss of life."

"I haven't heard a thing about any attacks," said Joe.

"You're damn right! That's because of our work and careful planning. Now, Joe, I want you to imagine the state of panic that would exist if these attacks were public knowledge. We'd have a total breakdown in our country. Do you understand that?"

"Yes," Joe said reluctantly.

"You see...it's not some theoretical threat...we've already been attacked. What's worse is that of all the people who have been directly exposed in these attacks, almost ninety percent have died, Joe. Antibiotics are useless. Our only hope is through immunization. Can you imagine how difficult it is to build a new vaccine in such a short time?"

Joe nodded.

"That's why we've had to use humans in our testing. We have *absolutely* no other choice, Joe. It may seem immoral at first glance, but it's absolutely necessary so we can protect the entire population. Now, for our testing, we're using already condemned people, men who need a chance to positively contribute to humanity. These men are being given one last chance to prove their value to God. The people that have been infected, Joe, are either on death row or have had at least three convictions for either violent crime or sex crimes, including child molesters. It's the best of a lot of bad possible choices. When asked, I volunteered to lead The Project. We chose Arkansas because on the off chance that a case was discovered outside of our Project, it wouldn't arouse much attention, because we've all seen some tularemia cases here in Arkansas. The one thing I didn't count on was one of my own students, whom I taught well, to be the one to stumble onto a leak."

Joe looked up from the floor.

"Okay Joe, now comes the *really* hard part. We simply cannot tolerate outside knowledge of the Project—not at all. Absolutely no exceptions. Which is what brings us to our current position. You're an example of just such outside knowledge. We also know you've involved others. One of the hardest decisions I've ever made was to have Brad Yates eliminated as an outside source."

Joe's head dropped.

"And the girl ..."

Joe stood and lunged at Dr. Bradley but was brought violently back to his seat by the men behind him.

"Sit down!" Dr. Bradley glared at Joe. "You will sit down and listen to me, Joe, or God help me, you will regret it."

Joe sat without further resistance.

"And the girl, as I was saying, is going to be detained. She will not be harmed because she has no proof of anything, just a story, but she can't be allowed to circulate, and above all else, she can't be allowed to investigate further. Someone has been sent to pick her up."

Dr. Bradley leaned back in his chair, folded his arms, and stared at Joe.

"Since you now know...I have two choices: eliminate you, or bring you inside The Project. I think everyone's interests are better served if you join our effort to fight this war."

"May I speak frankly, sir?"

"Of course."

Joe leaned forward.

"Dr. Bradley, I think you're insane."

Dr. Bradley's expression changed. He raised his eyes to the ceiling and sighed.

"I think your goals are admirable, but your actions are terrible," Joe said. "I cannot imagine how you compare soldiers dying on the beach at Normandy to prisoners being murdered in Arkansas. That comparison belittles the actions of those soldiers and their reason for dying."

"You forget that many of those soldiers were drafted and forced against their will to be killed at the barrels of those German guns."

"The fact that you don't get it, even now, scares me even more. There's no way you'll ever get me to work on this Project of yours. If you have to kill me like you did Brad, then go right ahead."

Dr. Bradley frowned. "This is a very sad day, very sad indeed. I was hoping that you could see things logically and pragmatically, not emotionally. I'll give you more time to think about it if you'd like. I warn you of one thing again. Don't force us to protect ourselves. We're not playing a game."

"You do what you have to do. I'm not playing your game."

Dr. Bradley nodded, and the two men seated behind Joe rose and grabbed him by his arms.

He leaned forward to Joe. "When we leave this office and this building, you *will* behave yourself. Your only hope of seeing tomorrow is to be calm. For the sake of everyone outside, these men can act like FBI agents, and I'll tell everyone that unfortunately you're being arrested for child pornography. When you don't come back, you'll be remembered as a kiddy porn freak. Let's go...quietly."

Dr. Bradley opened the door to the office and led them out. As they walked down the hall to the elevator, Dr. Moon stopped Dr. Bradley. "Sam, I'm sorry to interrupt you, but I need to ask you about the staff meeting."

"Sure, no problem," he said as they all stopped. "Go ahead to the elevators, and I'll meet you there."

As they walked to the elevator, Joe tried to think of any way to flee, but he had trouble focusing his thoughts. One of the men stepped in front of Joe to push the elevator button. He said nothing.

After waiting about thirty seconds, they heard Dr. Bradley walking down the hallway. As he turned the corner, he wasn't alone; a tall, overweight man dressed in a blue shirt and navy sport coat was behind him. They approached slowly, and the expression on Dr. Bradley's face had changed. He held his hands to his sides with his palms pointing towards the ground.

"Hey, pigs," the man in the navy coat said. "I suppose that you guys won't just let Joe go, so by the same token, I'll keep your Dr. Bradley."

The man in the navy coat seemed very calm. He turned Dr. Bradley slightly to the side revealing a gun aimed at his back.

"Now, two things are going to happen. First, you're going to take your guns out of their holsters and put them in the trashcan there. Second, you're going to move away from my friend and stand over there by the windows."

He pressed the barrel of the gun harder into Dr. Bradley's back.

The taller of the two men looked at Dr. Bradley. "Doctor S, what do you want us to do?"

"Let Joe go. We can pick him up before he's able to leave the campus. It's not a problem."

The two men slowly took out their guns and dropped them into the trashcan by the elevator and stepped back. Joe was free.

"Joe, push the down button. We're leaving these gentlemen now."

He eased the pressure between the gun barrel and Dr. Bradley's back.

When the elevator came, they backed into it, and just before the doors closed, the tall man shoved Dr. Bradley forward out onto the floor in front of the elevators.

"He's right," Joe said after the doors closed. "There's no way we're getting off this campus. He'll have it shut down to all traffic in about two minutes."

"I have ways."

"Who are you?"

"A friend of a friend," the man said. "That's all you need to know for now."

Joe looked at him intently. "Then you know Jules is in trouble, too."

"Yes. And we're going to get her...right now."

- seventeen -

Joe didn't understand how the situation was a significant improvement. He knew that Dr. Bradley was calling security to have them stopped. However, the man in the navy coat seemed able to muscle his way out of a jam. In all the excitement, the man had worked up a sweat, and his graying comb over had flapped down on his forehead.

"What are you going to do when these doors open and security is waiting on us?" Joe asked.

"Well, let's just say I have a plan. Jules told me that you might be in trouble, so I took the liberty of getting some help out of here."

"That makes me feel some better. By the way, who in the hell are you?"

"The name's Billy. We'll talk more later. Now listen, in order for all to go well, you must do everything I tell you to do."

He pointed his gun forward, and the elevator doors opened in the basement. As promised, no security guards awaited them. Billy peered out the doors to the left and stepped out into the empty hallway.

"Quick...we have to get through the kitchen."

"Why are we going to the kitchen?"

"I told you before. I don't have time to explain. Just trust me. Now, move!"

He pulled Joe forward down the hallway. They pushed through the double doors into the cavernous hospital kitchen, where the cooks were preparing the evening meals for eight hundred patients. Billy walked past the main prep line toward the stock area and went through two more doors into the loading dock, where boxes of produce were stacked to the ceiling. Joe saw an ambulance where two men in paramedic uniforms opened the rear doors. They jumped in the back, and the doors slammed behind them.

"Anybody here need a ride?" one paramedic said from the driver's seat.

"Love one," Billy said.

"Where to, chief?"

"Hit Markham Street towards downtown. Then I'll tell you where," Billy said as he lay down on the stretcher and covered up. "If we get stopped, doc, you need to break out your stethoscope and do some doctor shit."

"I get it," said Joe.

As the ambulance pulled onto the street, the campus police were setting up to block traffic, but they made no attempt to stop the ambulance. Once off campus, they turned east, towards downtown. They passed two Little Rock Police sedans speeding towards the medical campus.

The ambulance continued east on Markham Street, then turned left into a school parking lot. They stopped in the rear lot, obscured from view.

Billy jumped out the back doors.

"We get off here, doc."

"No problem," said Joe. "Whatever you say."

The paramedics remained in the front seats, and Billy shook hands with the driver. He laughed loudly and slapped the driver's shoulder.

"Can I thank them?" Joe asked.

"Not needed. They were doing me a favor. I did some work for the driver to get him out of some trouble."

Billy motioned for Joe to get into his car, an older model Ford Taurus with several dents on the passenger side. The inside wasn't much better, with several burn marks in the upholstery and the front floorboard covered with newspapers.

"Sorry for the mess, but I had to let my maid go," Billy said.

"I know what you mean. You just can't find good help, these days."

They both laughed.

Billy steered the car back out onto the street and turned left, towards downtown.

"Let's go get Jules."

They drove rapidly towards downtown and passed three more police cars speeding in the other direction.

Billy frowned. "I don't really know exactly who your Dr. Bradley is, but he sure has some pull...to be able to make one phone call and get this kind of response this quickly."

"You really have no idea," Joe said as he stared straight forward. "There's some pretty awful things going on."

"I know some of it," Billy said. "I went to Baltimore to visit your friend."

Joe turned to look at Billy.

"Jules sent me there to observe him, but when I got there, he was already dead."

"You saw him?"

"No, I saw the police tape at his apartment. I called back to Jules, and she told me what had happened. I don't know all of what's going on, but I see some bad things happening to good people."

"You got that right."

"One thing I can tell you, though. There's at least two people in the world you can trust with your life, doc."

"You cannot imagine how good that makes me feel right now."

As Billy drove, he frequently looked back through the rear-view mirror. Joe thought that this wasn't the first time Billy had been in a similar spot, which was reassuring.

"You know, Billy, I've done many things at work where I've had to make quick decisions that affect life and death."

"Yeah?"

"But right now, I can't even think straight. I know I need to calm down, but I can't."

"Just focus on what you have to do...what you have to do *right* now," Billy said. "Call Jules on her phone."

"I don't have her number."

"Take my cell phone," Billy said, handing his phone to Joe. "Just hit redial."

Joe hut the button. After several rings, he said, "I don't think she has it turned on."

Billy frowned. "Yes, she does. She's in trouble. She told me that she'd wait on my call, no matter what. If she isn't answering, then she can't answer. Damn it. I didn't plan for this."

"What do you think?"

"Well, we have to assume that Bradley planned this—to get Jules, I mean. He'll probably call in some heavy hitters, like the police or FBI. If we're going to take her, we have to have an element of surprise."

They arrived at the studio and circled the block. Billy parked the car one block away opposite the main entrance. A black sedan was parked in front of the studio with two men wearing business suits sitting in the front seat, waiting.

"That's a Federal sedan," Billy said. "Probably FBI. Damn it!"

"What do you think?" Joe asked.

"We wait."

After about ten minutes, the door opened. Two men in suits, each one holding an arm, walked with Jules towards the sedan. She held her head low, expressionless. The first man entered the rear door and moved across the seat. The second man forced Jules into the car with one hand on her head. The sedan eased forward into traffic. Billy pulled forward and circled back to follow, a few cars behind. The black sedan pulled into the left turn lane ahead of them. Billy quickly turned across traffic to the left one block behind them.

"Put your seatbelt on, doc. This is gonna get bumpy."

He raced forward, to get ahead of the black sedan. After five blocks, Billy veered to the right. Joe looked back to the right to see the sedan heading towards them. As Joe turned back to Billy to ask what his plan was, the Taurus lurched forward into the traffic. It struck the black sedan on the left front wheel and quarter panel. The sedan violently swung to its right side, with its forward progress deflected by the Taurus, and stopped sideways in the intersection.

"Get out and follow my lead. Go to the backseat near Jules. Tell them you're a doctor and need to check to see if everyone is okay. I'll make them give her up."

"What?" Joe yelled. "Are you crazy? These guys will kill us."

"Just do exactly what I say, Joe. Now!"

Billy pushed open his door and got out, walking calmly towards the sedan.

"Are you all right?" Billy asked as he approached the driver of the sedan.

The street was full of onlookers, startled by the noise of impact.

"I'm so sorry," Billy said. "I thought the light was green. I'm so sorry."

The dazed driver of the sedan got out of the car and stood up, arching his shoulders and back. The men in the backseat did not move. The man in the passenger seat got out and walked around to the driver's side.

Billy approached them. "I'm so sorry. Are you okay?"

Joe walked behind Billy. He looked at the backseat, then approached the door and opened it.

"I'm a doctor," he said. "I want make sure everyone is alright."

"We're fine," the agent said.

Joe looked at Jules. She appeared to be okay, only shocked to see him.

As Joe turned back, Billy reached into his coat and pulled out guns in both hands and pointed one at the center of the forehead of the driver and the other at the passenger who walked in front of the car. They both stopped with no attempt at resistance.

"Nobody move an inch," Billy yelled. "*You*...in the back seat. Put your hands on the seat in front of you, or I'll shoot your friends."

The two men, still shaken from the crash, complied.

"Turn around and put your hands on the car."

Billy waved his guns at the two men outside the car. They turned slowly and followed instructions.

"Take this," Billy said to Joe, handing him a gun.

Joe reluctantly took the gun and pointed it in the direction of the back seat, not knowing what to do.

"Now, nobody will get hurt here if you do exactly what we tell you to do. And the same goes for everyone else," Billy said, waving the gun at the people on the side of the street who were witnessing the event. "This is a police matter."

"You...in the back seat," Billy said. "Get out slowly and join your friends up here. Move slowly with your hands up."

Joe trembled as he pointed the gun.

The agent stood up from the backseat, as instructed. Billy shoved him up against the car.

"Now it's your turn," he yelled at the man on the far side of the car. "Get out slowly with your hands out front at all times."

Once all four men were lined up outside the car, Jules got out of the backseat.

"Here, take this," Billy handed his gun to Jules; she took it reluctantly. "Now, if anyone makes any sudden moves or decides to do something stupid, like be a hero, then they'll be shot right here."

Billy searched the agents. He took out pistols from each man's shoulder holster, then patted down each man. He also took the two agents' cell phones and crushed them on the asphalt.

"Now, each of you lie face down on the pavement with your hands to the side. Don't do anything stupid."

Billy motioned for Joe and Jules to go back to the Taurus. Jules got in the front seat next to Joe, but she could barely see over the crumpled front right fender.

"Joe, pull up here," Billy said as he stood over the agents.

He opened the right rear door and just before he got in the car, he fired his gun at the front and rear driver's side tires. The crowd of onlookers lowered to the ground as the shots rang out. After firing, Billy sat in the back seat and closed the door.

"Now drive," he said. "We have about ten minutes before this town is completely closed for business. Go south towards I-440."

Joe mashed on the accelerator, and the dented Ford Taurus lunged forward.

"By the way, remind me never to piss him off," Joe said to Jules.

"How did you...When did you...I don't understand," Jules stammered. "They marched straight into the studio and announced I was under arrest on Federal charges. They read me my rights and escorted me out. Everybody at the station froze with surprise, including me. That was unbelievable."

"Jules...I don't think I want any more jobs from you," Billy said as he laughed. "And this one is definitely gonna cost you extra."

- eighteen -

Joe followed the interstate highway to the north across the Arkansas River. At the first exit, they turned back to the east on a single-lane highway. After about twenty miles, they approached the town of England, Arkansas. They turned to the right on Haywood Street and stopped at a small brick house.

"Pull around the back," Billy said to Joe. "Let me out and I'll open the garage door."

"Who lives here, Billy?" Jules asked.

"This is my aunt's house. We'll be safe here for now."

Joe parked the dented Taurus in the small single car garage. They walked around outside, behind the red brick house. The house was relatively small, but the lot was large, about an acre. A small garden with straight rows was planted near the side, tended with great care. Billy closed the garage door concealing the Taurus inside, and the three travelers walked to the back door of the house and knocked.

After a few seconds, a frail gray-haired woman answered the door.

"Billy! It's so good to have you here," she said. "Who are your friends?"

"Hey, Auntie Ella," Billy said, with a kiss on the left cheek. "This is Jules."

He moved Jules forward.

"Oh, my. Aren't you a pretty thing?"

Jules smiled.

"And this is Joe," he said with another motion to move forward.

"Hello," Joe said politely. "It's very nice to meet you. We appreciate your hospitality."

They walked through the back door into the kitchen, a small room with old cabinetry and an even older gas stove. The décor was simple and clean, and the air faintly smelled of apples. Joe felt more relaxed.

"Are ya'll hungry...I can fix ya something to eat," she said.

"Maybe later. If you don't mind, I need to make a phone call," Billy said.

"Sure honey, you know where it is."

The silence was interrupted by a loud knock at the front door. Billy lunged in front of his aunt, shielding her.

"I'll get the door."

"Goodness. You act like someone is here to rob us. I mean really..."

"Please stay in here with Joe and Jules. I need to see who's at the door. I'll explain later."

Billy stared at Jules.

"Hey, if you don't mind, I could use a drink," Jules asked in a quiet voice. "What do you have?"

"Oh, pardon me for not offering," she said, temporarily distracted from Billy. "I have some lemonade, if that's okay?"

"That would be great."

"I agree," Joe said. "I haven't had a decent glass of lemonade in years."

"Well, that's just too long."

She reached for four glasses.

Billy walked into the living room and saw an outline of a man through the curtains. He pulled the curtains aside and saw a well-groomed man dressed in a blue golf shirt and khaki pants. He had black hair, graying above the ears and a large scar above his right eye.

"Can I help you?" Billy offered as he opened the front door slightly.

"No, but I can help you," the man said. "I know what kind of day you've had. We've been watching."

Billy shoved the front door back, but the man put his foot down in front of it.

"Stop! I'm not here to hurt you, but there are others around who will. I'm here to help you."

Billy stopped struggling against the door.

"Look, I'm alone here. I've been sent to help you. We were following Joe and Jules today and saw the fireworks."

The man let go of the door.

"I followed you here. Many of us want you to succeed. And I can tell you that there are many others who want you dead."

Billy stood motionless.

"If you'll let me inside to talk, I can make all of this much more clear."

Billy stepped aside to let the man through the door. As he moved forward, Billy shoved him face first into the open door. The man's body ·slammed into the door, sending a picture from the wall beside the door crashing to the floor. All of the noise brought Joe out from the kitchen to help.

"Look," the man struggled without success to free himself from Billy's hold. "This is not necessary. I'm alone and I'm not armed and I'm not here to hurt you."

"Joe, check him," Billy said, pressing the man firmly into the door.

Joe moved into the living room towards the struggle. The man against the door recognized the futility of trying to fight Billy. Joe approached the man cautiously and patted along his chest and legs for weapons, but found none.

"I don't find anything."

Billy freed the man, and he straightened his shirt as he walked across the room to sit down. Joe and Billy followed him.

"I'm sorry for the rudeness, but we're very paranoid at this point," Billy said.

"I understand," the man said, "and you should be paranoid. Unfortunately for you, I don't think you know the depth of the trouble you're in. The people that you've irritated won't stop until you're dead. They won't stop what they're doing because they're convinced it's in the interest of national security."

Jules walked out of the kitchen to listen, leaning on the doorway.

"We know several things, believe it or not," Joe said. "We know they're killing people...prisoners...in a twisted attempt to help others. We know that there's been some type of biological weapon developed, and there's a threat that it'll be released."

The man leaned back in the chair, listening to Joe.

"We know that powerful people are connected to Dr. Bradley. He seems to be the coordinator of this program."

"You honestly don't know shit, son," the man interrupted. "You think Bradley is the director. That's pretty far off the truth...the real director is the President of the United States, as Commander-In-Chief of the armed forces. That's the one calling the shots. That's the one ultimately responsible for what's going on. That's the one who ordered the Project into existence. That's the one you're fighting right now, not Dr. Bradley. And the Project demands that all three of you must be eliminated. You have a very big problem."

Joe stared at Jules, then down at the floor and took a deep breath.

"You're now officially public enemies number one, two, and three," the man continued. "You will have the full force of the Federal Government coming down on you—the FBI, the locals, the CIA…the works."

"Well, who the hell are you, mystery man?" Billy asked. "Who the hell are you to know all of this, and why are you telling us? None of it makes a damn bit of sense to me. Who do *you* work for?"

"I'm your new best friend. You can call me Nate. I represent a group that doesn't agree with the position of the President on this matter. We're very much opposed to the Project. I was sent to help you—to keep you alive. Unfortunately, I can't give you any material help. No money, no papers, no nothing. All I can offer is information, but information is more valuable than just about anything else in your world right now."

"Who do you work for?" Billy repeated.

"There's no way I can explain who I work for. There's no way you can understand it."

"What does that mean?" Joe said. "Try us—we're pretty smart people."

"Oh, we know you're smart, all of you. You've proven that. You've also proven that you're resourceful, which I guarantee will be a valuable asset in the next few days. I work for a branch of government that officially doesn't exist. We operate outside the mainstream. We exist, and have always existed in this country, to serve the President in gathering information and processing it so that the leaders in government, especially the President, can make good decisions. But, in times of war, the President takes more advice from the military than from us, which at times leads to very bad decisions, like the ones that have forced us all to where we are now."

Billy leaned back in his chair. "You see, Jules. This is what I've been saying for years. They're all spying on each other. I don't trust any of the bastards, including you, Nate...but I know that's not your name."

"None of that matters right now. You need to know about the Project. Stop me for questions, if you have any."

They all nodded in agreement.

"You already have some picture of the background. The Iraqi army developed a terrible bacteriological weapon in the late 1990's. They made a strain of *Francisella tularensis* that is airborne, environmentally stable, and resistant to virtually all antibiotics. The mortality rate of direct contact is suspected to be greater than ninety percent. They've confirmed this both in field exposure as well as in controlled exposure. We had an entire squad of soldiers in Iraq killed by this bug because of an accidental exposure. We've had four attacks on airports here in the States in the last three months. You see, the threat is not theoretical. The threat is very, very real."

"I've heard all of this," Joe said impatiently.

"I haven't," said Jules.

"A committee of scientific experts met at the request of the President several times within days of the attacks to form a consensus view of how to best respond to the threat. It was quite clear that our standard response to chemical or biological weapons threats was inadequate. As antibiotics are useless for this bug, the recommendation was to rapidly develop a vaccine. Therefore, the Project was born. Its stated goal is the development of, as quickly as possible, a vaccine. Because there's no treatment when exposed and it kills damn near anything it touches, we have no other option. My group's analysis was the same, but we've strongly opposed the methods. We feel quite strongly that other ways exist to achieve the same ends, without sacrificing additional human lives. However, our arguments have not held much weight against the pure pragmatism of the military mindset: a few may suffer to save many."

Jules sat next to Joe but remained silent.

"Now here is where it gets really bad. It has other parts…three divisions, operating essentially independent of each other. First is the Project itself, the scientific arm for development of the vaccine, with Dr. Bradley leading it. There's a second division, codenamed 'Owl,' the main intelligence-gathering arm. They have both FBI and CIA personnel tasked to this arm. Unfortunately, because of extreme secrecy, we know little about this part. We don't know who leads it. Only the President connects all of the dots. The last section is codenamed 'Viper,' and is charged with security for the project. We don't know if the President is even aware of this part. We think the CIA black ops is working independently. Any threats to the Project are managed through this. It's headed by a two-star Army general who is very experienced. We know of at least ten assassinations, one of which was your friend in Baltimore. I'm very sorry, Joe. They've certainly killed others, but we haven't been able to verify details."

Joe's heart sank again. Jules placed her hand gently on his back.

"You need to be aware that all three of your names will be submitted to Viper for elimination. That's why I'm here now. We must not allow that to happen."

Billy interrupted. "How do we know you're not here from Viper, as you call it, to kill us?"

"Trust me when I tell you this…when Viper calls, there is no warning, and there is no mess. They're very good at what they do. We know they've retained the services of a very efficient contract killer who works independently. He's nearly invisible. We know him only by the name of Mercury. He's never been successfully photographed, and we know essentially nothing about him, except that he's very expensive and very good at what he does. We suspect that he'll likely be contacted for the contract on all three of you."

"I want to throw up," said Jules.

Joe continued to stare at the floor. Billy remained fixed on Nate.

"We think your only chance for success and survival is to be very high-profile, but until you can bargain for your safety, you must remain invisible."

"And how do you propose we bargain?" asked Billy

"You've got to be able to prove what's going on, then take the Project public—air the whole thing out. When the general public is made aware of what's going on, they won't tolerate it. As very public whistle-blowers, you'll be untouchable."

Joe looked at Jules.

"I can help, but you have to get the information yourself. We cannot risk associating ourselves with you, but we have a shared interest in your success."

"This is crap," Billy said loudly. "Why can't you people help us in a meaningful way? If your group is so powerful, why can't you stop them yourselves? Why do we have to be the pawns in your little chess game? This is crap."

"We know this is hard to accept, but you must understand that we're only as powerful as we're allowed to be. If the President knew of this conversation, we would be shut down. We usually try to sway policy...not action. But, in this case, the President is making a tragic mistake...in our opinion."

"It's still crap," Joe added.

"I agree," said Nate, "but there's nothing I can do to change that. All I can do is try to guide you with the most powerful tool you have, which is information. Hard assets you have to get yourself."

"That's not a problem," said Billy.

"Like hell it's not a problem," Joe looked at Nate. "You're telling us that the entire Federal Government is out to catch us."

"Yes, that's correct," Nate said.

"Billy...we're dead! We have no money, no way to travel, they know who we are, and what we look like. They know our addresses, our bank accounts, and our credit cards. They know everything about us. We're dead. There's no way we can escape this." Joe looked back at Nate. "How are we supposed to prove anything about the Project, when we can't even get basic information about it? And if we show up anywhere, we'll be arrested and thrown away like trash. We're dead."

Joe looked again at the floor.

"You're not exactly correct, Joe," said Billy. "They may know who *you* are, *your* address, *your* bank account, *your* credit cards and everything about *you*, but they don't know anything about me."

"What are you saying, Billy? They know everything about you, too. They know everything about everybody. It's unbelievable."

"Listen to him, Joe. Billy, here, is the invisible man."

Billy looked at Nate intently. "What do you know?"

"We don't know anything about you, Billy, and we've looked."

Billy smiled.

Nate laughed. "Explain it to Joe."

"I'm a paranoid son of a bitch, Joe. Jules can tell you. I do everything in cash. I have no bank accounts, no credit cards, no real address as far as these guys are concerned. I'm simply a name and a social security number and barely that. I hate the government and I don't trust any of them...ever since I got out."

"I'm afraid to ask, what do you mean...got out?" Joe said. "If I have to hear another far-out story, I'm afraid I'll lose it."

"Sit down, Joe," said Jules. "You might lose it."

"Ah shit, Jules. You mean you're living the secret life, too. Am I the only normal person in this room?"

"No, Joe. I'm as normal as anyone," Jules said, "but I know more about Billy. He used to be a lawyer but served time in a Federal prison for some mistakes."

"What mistakes...what is this?" Joe asked.

"Joe, I thought I could make some easy money in a real estate deal in northern Arkansas. My partners and I worked the deal for over a year. We all should have made money, but the banker got greedy, and the whole thing blew up. Federal investigators got involved, and I got sold out. The others had good political connections, so what the Feds didn't have in actual evidence, they made up. But it's really hard to prove when the government's lying. My partners moved on, and I moved out...to prison...for two years."

"Who were your partners?" Joe asked.

"Let's just say they've moved on to bigger and better things and leave it at that. I kept some of the money we made, and I keep it safe, but I don't trust anyone...especially the government."

"How much money?"

"Enough to help, but not enough to quit working."

Jules interrupted, "I met him in Dallas, when he was working there doing some freelance private investigator work. And I started him on steady work for our stories when I was at WFAA. We had a talent for getting into trouble together."

"She's the main reason I'm back in Little Rock," Billy said. "I've continued my investigative work, but I never let my guard down."

Nate laughed.

"What are you laughing at?" said Jules.

"We were trying to figure out how, or more importantly why, someone like Billy is invisible. This explains a whole lot. You guys are in better shape than I thought."

"Joe, we can take care of ourselves better than you think," said Billy. "I have money, I have a place to live that's quiet and untraceable, and I can get transportation. We can get started, but you and Jules have to stay out of sight. They don't know who I am. I should be alright."

"He's right, Joe," Nate said. "Nobody knows who he is. They have no pictures, no ID…nothing. Your name probably isn't even Billy, is it?"

"It is as far as you should know," said Billy.

"Outstanding," said Nate. "I can be contacted by e-mail at this address." He scribbled an address on a scrap of paper. "I suggest using only public computers from anonymous accounts to use this address."

"We know what to do," said Billy.

"Great." Nate stood up to leave, but as he walked out the door, he added, "Remember, you'll all be under contract for elimination. Be careful and be aware."

Joe sat on the couch, looking down, trying to collect his thoughts with all of the new information.

"I can't think straight with all of this. I just don't..." Joe stopped and frowned. "Last week, I was planning for a job and a place for a good round of golf. Now I just want to survive the day. No offense to you guys, but I don't know who I can trust."

"We have to get moving," Billy said as he closed the front door behind Nate. "This place is definitely not safe for us anymore. We need to get lost."

"I hope you know what to do and where to go, Billy, because I'm all out of ideas," Jules said.

Billy walked to the door. "I have a very good idea where to go next, but I need to get a clean car. I'll take care of this, but it'll take about thirty minutes. You guys should stay here."

"No problem." Jules moved towards the window to look outside. She turned back and motioned towards the kitchen. "What about your aunt? Will she be okay?"

"She's fine. She doesn't know anything about anything. Worst case, I guess, is she'll be questioned, but she'll be fine. They have no reason to do anything to her. Make sure you don't say anything about what's really going on."

Joe stared at the ceiling with his hands clasped behind his head.

Jules looked back at Joe. "Are you going to be okay?"

"Oh, I'll be fine. I just don't like being the center of attention. Especially to a bunch of people who want to kill me. Other than that, I'm perfect. Just perfect."

"I'll be back," Billy said.

Billy walked towards the kitchen to go out the back door as his aunt walked through the doorway from the kitchen carrying a platter with four glasses of lemonade.

"Alright. Sorry for the wait, but I had to make it fresh."

She walked slowly, careful not to spill a drop, unaware of what had just happened in the living room of her house.

She looked up at Billy, Jules, and Joe. They all laughed, relieved at her oblivion.

- nineteen -

As the sun worked its way through the blinds, a pattern emerged on the desk—bands of alternating light and shadow. The reports lay strewn across the desk. The results were all positive: what they were expected to be. Dr. Bradley had thoughts again of the objectives of the Project. When the President asked him to lead the Project, its existence seemed right, seemed necessary even. However, with a job of such complexity and breadth, the human side couldn't be avoided. The existence of Viper and its demons were understandable from the detached viewpoint of utilitarian necessity, but its true benefit was harder to find, a less than human part of a distinctly human endeavor.

He knew that Joe would pursue the case until he found the truth. He also knew that the work of the Project couldn't be made public; Joe couldn't be allowed to disclose the truth. The thought of involving Viper to intervene in this case made him consider again the overall purpose of the Project. He remembered when the President said that the purpose was to protect Americans and the American way of life. It sounded great in generality, but its application to the end was much more difficult.

He leaned across the desk and pressed the intercom button.

"Mildred, could you get Tom Henderson on the phone for me?"

He reviewed the reports again while he waited.

"Tom Henderson is on the phone, sir," Mildred said after a brief pause. "Shall I put him through to you?"

"Yes Mildred, thanks."

Dr. Bradley picked up the receiver. "Tom?"

"Hey, Sam, good to hear from you. What makes you call in the middle of the day? Usually we don't review until Fridays. What's up?"

"We have a major problem, and I need to talk to a friend, you know, someone I can trust."

"Sam, you sound serious. What's happened?"

"I have a major security problem."

Tom paused. "What sort of security problem?"

"There's no problem with you, Tom. I have a major leak that needs to be fixed, but it involves good people. They stumbled onto the Project by accident. Overall, they're essentially innocent bystanders in this whole nightmare, and I've tried every way I know to protect them, but they know far too much and they feel threatened. I tried to secure them physically, per protocol, but they escaped. They're now on their own, and I have no way to find them. Protocol says that I must notify Viper, but I know the outcome. It's not right."

"I understand...but as you explained to me when you brought me into this, we're making very tough decisions. We can't lose sight of the larger picture. What we're doing will be judged in those larger terms. We cannot sway from the primary goal: protecting our families, our country. You told me early on that we'd face tough choices. This is exactly what you were talking about. You just need to follow your own advice—keep your focus on the big picture. Do the right thing."

"You're a good friend, Tom. You're a good head to have. I'm just having problems seeing the larger picture at times like this."

"Damn right it is. This is what the terrorists are counting on...our weakness. They don't think we have the stomach to fight the fight to win."

Dr. Bradley paused again, silent on the phone.

"Sam, make the call to Viper and then forget it. It's done. This is why Viper exists—to separate the jobs, so the Project will succeed. Make the call, Sam."

"I will, Tom. Thanks for hearing me out."

"You bet. I'm always here. Now, as your own physician, I must recommend treating your depression. How does 7:30 sound tonight? Fajitas and margaritas?"

"Sounds good, Tom. I'll see you then."

He stared at the phone for a while and reflected on the intensity of the moment. With the next call, he was condemning people to death. He picked up the receiver and dialed.

◆ ◆ ◆

He received his instructions via e-mail and reviewed the attached files that included a brief background and general information on his targets—three of them. One was a young man, age twenty-eight, a doctor. The other was a woman, age twenty-nine, a reporter. The third was listed only as an unknown accomplice. Pictures of both the young man and woman were attached, but there was no picture of the third target. Also included were last known addresses, known associates, and family members, all with addresses and phone numbers.

He replied, "To be done. Mercury."

He checked his bank and verified that one-third of his fee had been deposited into his account. Because the contract included three targets and their location was unknown, the charge was more; the first deposit was $4 million. He reviewed the remainder of the information and planned his trip to the United States.

In the past, it was easier to make contacts and get continued support for information. It was always expensive, but with the heightened security, personal contact and intelligence were much more difficult, so he had changed his strategy. Since the introduction of Homeland Security, most intelligence was effectively collated there: from the FBI, CIA, INS, and DEA. While personal contact was more difficult, accessing the raw information was actually easier.

About two years earlier, Mercury had found one of the most lucrative contacts for information he had ever made: the vice-chief of information services for Homeland Security, John Dunhill. A long-time IBM and Microsoft employee, he had been recruited from the private sector to head the information exchange coordination between the various departments. His section was relatively small, with only thirty-one people tasked to it, but the work was important. Mercury had considered targeting a lower-level employee but decided against that strategy as that person's value would be shorter-lived; he needed a long-term arrangement. He was surprised that only three meetings were needed to arrange the information exchanges.

Dunhill created a new employee position with the department, hired to test security for the network, which Mercury filled under an assumed identity. Each time he needed information, Dunhill gave him basic network information, which made intrusion easy. The staff always discovered the intrusion, but information leakage resulted. Through one contact, he had access to nearly all vital data from United States intelligence-gathering activity as it was collated through the Department of Homeland Security.

He accessed the Internet, again through an anonymous wireless network, and connected to the extranet of the Department of Homeland Security. An automated program deciphered the administrative password and enabled Mercury to connect to the internal network of the department. He navigated to the FBI section and searched there for basic data on his contacts.

He found the psychological profiles of the targets. The first was the doctor. After extensive FBI interviews of friends and co-workers, the profilers performed an estimated Kuder test, which identified him as well-suited to his profession as a physician. The profile also included an estimated MMPI, a personality screening test, which identified him as elevated Scale 0, socially introverted, slightly elevated Scale 9, hypomania, and slightly elevated Scale 7, psychasthenia. Mercury looked at the descriptions. Hypomania implied rapid cycling between a depression and manic-type behavior. Psychasthenia implied obsessive-type behavior. The investigators found that his parents had been absent from his life since he was sixteen years old, which the profilers thought made him strongly independent and absolutist in moral values.

The second target was the twenty-nine-year-old woman, well-suited to her profession as a journalist. Her MMPI results were similar to the first target: elevated Scale 0, socially introverted, slightly elevated Scale 9, hypomania, and moderately elevated Scale 2, depression, thought to be due to the recent death of her mother. The results were likely not valid, the files reported, because of few interviews with co-workers and friends.

The third target was nearly blank, from a report standpoint. No known contacts were found. Kuder testing and MMPI testing were impossible. The investigators suspected that he was using a false identity, and full testing would be done when his real identity became known.

Financial analysis revealed that the first two contacts had little wealth overall. The young man had less than $5,000 total liquid net worth, and the woman had between $15,000 and $20,000 estimated liquid net worth. The investigators knew that with little cash or equivalents and few personal contacts, they couldn't support themselves for very long. The third target was completely unknown. The investigators viewed him to be the greatest potential problem. Financial analysis was impossible, so it wasn't clear whether he could provide resources for the other two.

The only direct contact with Federal agents showed that the three worked fairly well as a team. The older man, the unknown man, was the leader, which made Group Dynamic Analysis very difficult. Because the younger man and the woman both tested high on the socially introverted scale, they might take action at times independent of the others, which could serve as a stress point on the relationships. The analysts emphasized this point as a weakness of the group, a point that could be useful in negotiating, if necessary.

Ever since the woman had been freed from Federal custody by the other two, their locations were unknown, but they were assumed to be together. Homeland Security tasked itself to use all resources to locate them. Local and county law enforcement officials were given full identifying information, and a press release had already been completed. Mercury knew that it was unlikely that they would remain hidden for long. He would continue to monitor intelligence regularly.

◆ ◆ ◆

Billy returned to the house driving a white Ford F-150 truck with a raised suspension and large mud flaps.

"Where in the hell did you get that?" Joe said as he walked out the front door.

"Up the block to the fine gentlemen at the England Motor Company. I always enjoy dealing with a used car dealer when I walk in with cash. I promise you, if you've never done that, you're missing out on a treat," Billy said.

"Where did you get the cash?" Joe asked.

"I keep a stash here at my aunt's place for emergencies." Billy said.

"I don't even want to know what you paid for it."

Joe laughed at the sight of the truck.

"I gave six thousand four hundred dollars."

"That piece of junk isn't worth half that."

"Yeah, well, what they didn't know is that it's worth double that to us right now."

"True, true." Joe laughed harder.

"We need to get going," Billy said, motioning to the truck.

"Where do you suggest we go?"

"I have a place north of here that's quiet. It's just outside of Jasper, where Highway 74 comes off of Highway 5 going northwest out of town. It'll keep you two safe, as long as you stay low."

"How far is it from Little Rock?" Joe asked.

"It's a little over two hours, give or take."

"That's redneck country, isn't it?" Jules asked.

"Damn straight, and ya'll will fit in well with us."

"The truck will blend in well, too," Joe said.

Billy went back inside. His aunt stood in the kitchen washing some dishes.

"We're gonna go now. I'm sorry to leave so quickly."

"Billy…but you just got here. What about your friends?"

"It's okay. We're all going together. I need to take care of them and get them settled in."

"When will you come back for dinner and stay awhile?"

"Real soon. I promise."

"But, Billy…"

"Listen for a minute. Some people may come by and ask you questions. You can answer them any way you want."

"What do you mean?"

"I'm not sure. But if somebody comes by to ask about me, it's okay to tell them anything you want."

"Whatever. But I don't understand…"

"I'll see you later."

"Do ya'll want something to eat to take with you?"

"No, it's okay."

Billy walked back out the front door and got into the truck where Jules and Joe were waiting.

They drove in circles in the town and then again in North Little Rock to ensure that they were not being followed. Once Billy felt comfortable, they set out to the west and then northward. The drive took almost three hours ending on the winding roads of Highway 7 near Jasper, Arkansas. Normally, it was a fantastic drive with its views of the mountains, but they didn't notice the scenery. They were all tired, and as the sun was setting they needed a place to rest.

They arrived just before sunset. The house was small, only four rooms, shaped like a traditional log cabin with the roof crest parallel to the front of the house. A large porch extended outward beyond the front wall, inviting guests to the front door. They parked the white truck and went inside.

The interior was clean and well organized. The front door opened into a fairly large room. To the left was a small galley kitchen and to the right was the living room. A large fireplace built from small round rocks worn smooth from a local stream flanked the right wall.

"How did you get this place?" Joe asked.

"I built it myself," Billy said.

"You what?"

"I built it myself. It took a little over two years, but everything you see, I did myself." Billy moved into the kitchen and opened the refrigerator door. "This is my real home, not in the city."

"Really, Billy," Jules said, "I didn't know you had it in you."

"I need to go into town and stock you guys up on some groceries so you don't have to leave the house. You'll need to keep completely out of sight."

Billy grabbed the keys and walked towards the front door.

"Thanks, Billy. For everything," Jules said.

"No problems, guys. We just need to hold out a while longer so I can go to work and get some info on our good friend, Dr. Sam Bradley."

Billy walked out the door and drove away in the truck.

- twenty -

Joe explored the cabin as Jules picked up a magazine from the rustic coffee table, an old *National Geographic* from June 2001, and read an article about Pearl Harbor. She read about Navy divers disarming torpedoes in the sunken ships in total darkness because the leaking oil from the ships completely blocked sunlight. She was surprised to see a present day picture that showed oil still leaking from the sunken ships.

"Look at this, Joe," Jules said.

"What?"

"Oil is still leaking from the boats in Pearl Harbor. That's amazing," she said as she turned the page.

"I had this patient at the VA. He was a rear gunner on the battleship *Pennsylvania* docked across the Harbor from Battleship Row where the *Arizona* was. He actually saw the *Arizona* blow up...said it was the most unbelievable thing he'd ever seen. The *Oklahoma* took two or three torpedoes before it listed, right there in front of him. He saw sailors who were on fire diving into the water only to be machine gunned from the air by the Japanese planes. He said he hadn't seen anything like that until September 11, when those people were jumping out of the Trade Towers to die...took him right back to that day at Pearl Harbor."

"I've never been to Pearl Harbor," Jules said softly.

"Me neither," Joe replied as he walked over to sit down next to Jules.

They looked at the pictures together: picture after picture of battleships and carriers on fire.

"Joe?"

"Yeah?" he replied, still looking at the pictures.

"This whole thing that we're in the middle of seems like what your patient said."

"What do you mean?"

"I mean, with all we've gone through the past couple of days, it seems like we have a front row seat as a new Pearl Harbor happens, like September 11," Jules said.

"You mean because of Dr. Bradley?"

"No, I mean the people who want to attack us with that bacteria. If they were to succeed in releasing a bunch of that stuff in the middle of a city or a mall or something like that, it could kill thousands of people. I mean, the world would never be the same. It would be like after Pearl Harbor, or September 11."

"Yeah, it might," Joe said.

"I don't want this to sound bad, but I need to say this. Maybe Dr. Bradley and what he's doing isn't so terrible, I mean, if it's true that there's absolutely no other way…"

"No way, Jules. I can't believe there's any way that what he's doing is okay. Believe me, I understand how bad it can be. I sat helplessly and watched those prisoners die. I won't forget it, ever. What I can't get out of my head is what those prisoners' mothers were told. What about their family? What lies were told to them that made it all okay? No way, Jules, I don't care what they did to get into prison. It's just not right to make them suffer like that."

"I know what you're saying, but what are we supposed to do—just sit and wait for an attack on a big city?"

Joe stared out the window behind the couch. "I don't know what the right answer is either. But I feel like I know what the *wrong* answer is. Dr. Bradley said that he has to make 'hard choices'. But who is he to play God? How can any of us do that?"

"We can't, but it's not an unreasonable argument. You know, a few people sacrifice to…" She looked intently at him. "I just don't know."

"My problem is who decides who lives and who dies. Particularly when you're saying that the people who die get no choice, none at all."

"These guys we're talking about didn't seem to care about choice when they victimized people," Jules said.

"Yeah, that's right, but where does it stop? I mean, do you say it's okay to do this sort of thing to somebody that robbed a bank, you know, armed robbery, or whatever? If the threat were to get worse, it's a short distance along the 'greater good' line of thinking to allow stuff like this on shoplifters. You know, we have laws against cruel and unusual punishment. They're there for a reason."

Joe stood up from the couch to walk into the kitchen. He opened several cabinets.

"What are you looking for?"

"A glass. I'm thirsty."

"I saw some cups on the second shelf, there, on the left."

Joe opened the left cabinet. He got a glass down, filled it with water, and took a slow drink.

"I know you're right," Jules said as she got up to walk into the kitchen. "I just want all of this to end."

"So do I." he said as he put his arm around her shoulder and kissed her. "I want all of this to be over, too."

They stood in the kitchen in each other's arms, rocking slowly from side to side.

"You know, all of this is going to be like the *Arizona* in Pearl Harbor."

"What do you mean?" Joe asked.

"The oil is still coming up from that boat, and that was more than sixty years ago. The same will happen here, you know, the effects of all of this will still be visible sixty years from now. I wonder what people then will say about all of this."

"I don't know. I just don't know."

Joe stared out the window.

They walked over to the couch and lay down. They said nothing, and after a short while, both were asleep.

Joe jumped at the sound of the door opening. Billy was struggling with several plastic bags.

"Here, grab these," Billy said, handing several bags to Joe. "Put them over there on the counter."

"Damn, man, how much stuff did you get? This looks like we're loading down for the whole winter."

Jules got up from the couch to help. She took a couple of bags from Joe and walked into the kitchen. She began unloading the bags as Joe and Billy walked outside to get others out of the truck.

Joe followed Billy.

"It's worse than I thought," said Billy.

"What do mean?"

"You guys can't leave here at all."

"What?" Joe said as he stopped.

"I went down into town, and your pictures are everywhere on the TV." Billy leaned on the side of the truck. "They have you two pegged for the supposed attack on Federal agents in Little Rock."

"I can't believe it," Joe said as he kicked at a rock on the ground.

"I sat and watched CNN as they described the attack on four Federal agents who were investigating a terrorism link in Little Rock. They said they were injured while attempting to question an associate of a doctor who works as a resident physician at the VA Hospital."

"I can't believe it."

"You better believe it. You also better damn sure stay here and be invisible. There's no place you can show your face now...not even in isolated Jasper, Arkansas. This is craziness."

Billy lifted the rest of the sacks from the truck bed and walked towards the cabin. Joe remained at the truck.

"Are you coming inside, Joe?" Billy asked as he walked up the stairs.

"Just give me a minute."

"Alright."

After a few minutes outside, Joe walked up the front steps back into the cabin. Billy and Jules unpacked the groceries.

"Billy said he bought enough groceries for about ten days. You have to put up with me for ten straight days," Jules said. She turned and looked at Joe. "What's wrong?"

"Did Billy tell you about the store?"

"No." Jules turned towards Billy. "Why...what happened at the store?"

"Well, as I told Joe, you guys are gonna have to stay here absolutely out of sight until we can get things, um, corrected."

"Really? I thought that being up here in the middle of nowhere was enough."

Joe walked over to the kitchen cabinet. "Apparently, it's all over the news that we attacked Federal agents in Little Rock."

Jules dropped the jar of peanut butter that she was holding.

"Yeah, they said Federal agents were investigating a terrorism link to a medical resident at the VA and that we attacked them. We're supposedly loose and considered armed and dangerous."

Billy continued to put the groceries away.

"So my whole station...everyone at work now thinks that the agents that picked me up were taking me because I was involved in a Federal agent's assault?"

"Yup," said Billy. "Even better, though, is the story of how you escaped, with the help of your accomplices."

Jules walked over to sit on the couch.

"You two characters are now front and center. I'll tell you guys something. This whole Project that you're mixed up in must go all the way to the top, like that guy, Nate, said. At first, I didn't really believe him, but now I think he was talking straight."

Joe walked over and sat next to Jules. "Now how do you feel about the whole thing?"

"Terrible," Jules said. "I've spent my whole damn life to get to where I'm at now, and these bastards take it from me in a single day. I haven't done anything wrong— nothing at all."

"This is what I was talking about, Jules. The longer this thing goes on, the more people will be hurt. It's not just murderers and rapists who get hurt. It's a big damn nightmare when you start taking away people's basic right to be left alone. That's all I want right now. I just want to be left alone."

Billy walked out of the kitchen.

"Listen, guys. I think we can do this. They have no idea who I am. I can move pretty freely. I just need to get us a much stronger hand to play in this poker game. I'm sure we can put the squeeze on this whole thing because believe it or not, we have the advantage."

"Honestly, I don't really see how we have the advantage," Joe said.

"We have the advantage because what they're doing to the prisoners *is* wrong. All we have to do is air it all out—get it out in the public eye. Nobody will stand for it. This bullshit story will look a lot different once the whole thing is aired out."

"You may be right that this will look different under the light of day. But when you're stuck under the shoe of the giant, it's a little difficult to see the sunshine," Jules said.

"Come on, Jules. If anyone likes a David and Goliath story, it's you."

Jules stood up and walked towards the kitchen. "I'd like to see all of this wide open, just to see the bastards squirm. I could get some pleasure out of that."

Joe interrupted. "Both of you are forgetting something. We have no help, except each other. Goliath is really, really big, and David is really, really small."

"Yeah, but it'll be all the better when the giant falls." Jules said.

"Joe, my friend, have more faith in the giant killer here," Billy said as he tugged at his shirt. "You're asking me to do what I do best, which is gather information. You know, we don't have to invent anything. All we have to do is gather the truth and then air it out."

♦ ♦ ♦

Mercury sat at the table and looked over the saved pages. As he moved from page to page, he saw nothing that was helpful. He scanned the best two sources: the FBI counterintelligence communications and the Homeland Security communications. With Google's search technology now available for the internal network searching, it was much simpler to search for any reports tagged with the names of Joe Mason or Jules Green. By this time they both had FBI case numbers that made searching easier. He saw a considerable amount of activity within the FBI in attempting to locate them. The story about the assault on Federal agents was obviously false, but he thought it was a fairly bold move to try to find them. It was also interesting that they would do this at the same time that his services were requested.

The FBI was using their traditional technique of concentric-ring locating. The technique worked in that the investigators started with the missing suspect at the center, then they located people closest to them: family, friends, and co-workers. If nothing of use was found, they then expanded the ring of contacts to include more and more people, eventually connecting even quite remote acquaintances at the outermost rings of contact. The technique generally worked well as long as continual pressure was applied. Mercury thought that the technique should work well for this case, but he was somewhat concerned that he might have difficulty in getting to them before they were arrested. It would be much more difficult to complete the contract, and get paid, if they were in Federal custody—difficult, but not impossible.

After about thirty minutes of scanning, it was clear that the suspects were still at large. He would wait, scanning the intelligence at least three times daily. He knew that he would have to move quickly once any information was found, so he had traveled to Little Rock and booked a room at the downtown Capital Hotel. He loved this type of hotel—older, thick with tradition, with luxurious accommodations and top-level service. He traveled disguised as a bond-trader who would meet with private bankers at Stephens, Inc. in Little Rock, the largest investment-banking firm not located in New York City.

The small coffee shop down the street from the hotel was quaint and private. He found three different open wireless networks that he could use for Internet access. The best one came from an exercise studio above the coffee shop. With so much open access, Mercury was able to stay close to the hotel, and his car, but still maintain secrecy in his work.

- twenty one -

After two days of close monitoring, Billy was able to deduce Dr. Bradley's basic daily routine. Early in the morning, he would go out his front door and get the morning paper, The *Arkansas Democrat-Gazette*. He would then go out to his back porch and read the paper outside while sipping morning coffee. About thirty minutes later, his wife joined him taking the sections he had already read. She wasn't, it appeared, a coffee drinker as the last two mornings she had had orange juice. She seemed taller than Billy had expected, as tall as Dr. Bradley, but that fact was somewhat difficult to tell from the distance from which he was observing.

After a twenty-minute jog followed by a shower, Dr. Bradley left his home in the Heights neighborhood of Little Rock for the short drive down to the campus. He parked his silver Chevy Tahoe in his assigned spot in the parking garage across from the Stephens Neurosciences Building. He then walked across the street and entered the ground floor of the

VA Medical Center. He checked briefly with his research laboratory on the ground floor and then took an elevator to the sixth floor and started his day from his office there. His workday was somewhat variable, between making rounds on patients and working some in a clinic on the first floor of the building. He spent some time the second day in a staff meeting at the University Hospital across the street, but it was fairly brief.

After work ended, which was 6:30 p.m. on day one and 7:15 p.m. on day two, he drove the same route north on Kavanaugh Boulevard to his home. Shortly after arriving home, he would have a couple of drinks with his wife prior to eating dinner.

Billy had carefully placed three listening devices on three windowpanes outside the house that served as excellent sources of audio information from inside the house. In addition, he had placed an additional device on the rear passenger window of Dr. Bradley's car along with a GPS tracking device underneath the passenger's seat. Curious, he thought, Dr. Bradley doesn't lock his car at night—perhaps he feels secure in the upscale area of Little Rock.

The third day was different. After his usual check-in with his laboratory, which took about thirty minutes, he drove southward out of Little Rock towards Pine Bluff, Arkansas. After about thirty miles, he exited along a small state highway. After about a mile southward, he turned left into the Pine Bluff Arsenal. Billy parked his white truck slightly up the road, out of sight. He had a strong GPS signal on Dr.

Bradley's SUV. After about two hours, Dr. Bradley re-emerged from the gate and turned south. As they drove past, Billy noticed a second person in the SUV. He followed about a quarter mile back, keeping track with the GPS locator and a map linked on a laptop. He listened as best he could to the conversation.

"...I met with her two days ago to discuss the timeline. We've moved production schedules to continue to deliver...through next week." Billy listened closely but the road noise made the voices difficult to hear.

"That's fine...still got to complete all of the phase three...submit to CDC in Atlanta and...for...Detrick."

"I told her...you...almost finished and that she'd have everything documented...insisted...start distribution early. Sh...didn't have time."

"I know...saw the report..."

"How long...it'll take to get everyone inoculated?"

"...three weeks...guess, but complete blackout...public knowledge."

"...agree. I don't think...shorter than that."

"Military and Federal teams...already done..."

The road noise covered the remainder of the conversation. Billy couldn't hear any better while driving. He knew that the recording software on his computer could help clarify the recording. Joe could hear it all better when played back. Perhaps it would make more sense.

The silver Tahoe stopped in Pine Bluff just off 13th street for lunch at Arthur's Bar-B-Q, which, judging by the number of patrons, seemed to be a good place to eat.

After about forty minutes, the pair of men got back into the car and turned back west and left town southward on Highway 79. After about ten miles, they turned left, drove for another two miles and turned left again up a dirt road. Billy stayed back on the main road and watched.

The silver Tahoe made its way up the dirt road to a fairly large bland-appearing building. From the road, the building looked like a small metal warehouse. The Tahoe moved around the rear of the building and stopped. Billy couldn't see anything from his position on the road. He parked his truck and walked across the road towards the building. He wanted to get a closer look at the rear of the structure.

A small wire fence separated the property from the roadway. As Billy approached it, he stopped. He noted that the fence was quite shiny, not what he expected from an old wire fence. As he looked cautiously around, he could see a remote viewing camera, which was mounted unobtrusively in a nearby tree, moving slowly from side to side. He ducked behind a shrub as it turned in line with his position.

He looked in the other direction and saw another camera about fifty yards down the road. It was also concealed, making it very unlikely that any casual passersby would it. Likely, he thought, the area had perimeter alarms that signaled any intruders. Billy thought he had moved too close, so he waited for the camera to aim in the other direction and walked back across the roadway to his truck. He drove down the road a short distance, turned around, and waited for the Tahoe to start moving again.

After about three more hours, the silver Tahoe pulled out from around the rear of the building and turned to the right off of the dirt road back onto the highway. Billy noticed that now Dr. Bradley appeared to be alone. He followed the Tahoe, at a distance, toward Little Rock.

After the short drive back to Little Rock, Dr. Bradley turned west on I-630, cutting through the center of the city from east to west. At 5:15 in the evening, rush-hour traffic filled the westbound lane. Billy followed the silver Tahoe as it turned to the right, back northward past several shopping strip malls, and into a neighborhood of medium-sized conservative homes. Once through the neighborhood, the Tahoe parked at a restaurant, and Dr. Bradley went inside. Billy parked across the street and waited.

After about an hour inside the restaurant, Dr. Bradley emerged talking to a smaller man with sandy-blond hair. He was older than Dr. Bradley and appeared to be very athletic and thin, like a long-distance runner. The man looked familiar. Billy drove out of the parking lot across the street in order to get a closer look at the man with Dr. Bradley and recognized him; it was Jules's boss, the manager at her television station. Billy had met him a few times with Jules.

Dr. Bradley then drove back home. Billy sat outside and listened but heard no discussions about the day's activities.

Dr. Bradley's wife asked the typical question of "How was work, honey?" which was followed by "Fine, not much new."

Billy followed for two additional days and saw very little change in the typical routine. He sent an e-mail to Nate, saying he wanted to meet, privately, to discuss and verify information. Billy was surprised that the e-mail was answered in minutes. They agreed to meet in Little Rock, the following morning, at the Farmer's Market downtown, a bustling open-air market.

Billy arrived at the Farmer's Market about fifteen minutes early and parked his truck facing forward in a space adjacent to the public library. He walked slowly across President Clinton Avenue and looked eastward to see the Presidential Library. The Market was busy, as many locals filled the tent-like structure to buy and sell fresh vegetables. Billy perused the selection of corn, in husks, vine-ripened tomatoes, and was particularly intrigued by the melons.

"Are these honeydews?" he asked.

"Picked yesterday. They's sweet...had some this mornin' fo' breakfast," the elderly lady behind the table said. "Can I wrap up a couple for ya?"

"Not right now, thanks. I'm just looking, but I'm sure I'll be back."

"Well...don't wait too long, 'cause these usually don't last long."

"Understood, ma'am."

Billy smiled at the lady. He turned around and looked back across the Arkansas River and was startled when he felt a tug on his shoulder.

"Hello, Billy."

"Hey, Nate. What's with the suit? You look like a lawyer," Billy said.

"Look around. Suits are all around here. You called and said you had some questions. What have you found?"

Billy turned to walk towards the river, and Nate followed.

"I've been tracking Dr. Bradley. He's been busy."

"Yes," Nate said.

"I tracked him to the Pine Bluff Arsenal. I assume that they have some kind of facility there."

"Yes, they do. That's where the main laboratories and meeting areas are located. The bulk of the research happens there. It's been used like that for a long time."

Nate turned toward Billy with his back to the river.

Billy frowned. "Then I followed him to a small warehouse-type building south of Pine Bluff. I tried to get closer for a look, but it seemed to be secured pretty tight, with some pretty expensive gear that was well concealed."

"That was a good find," Nate smiled. "That's the main experimental lab, where they take the subjects for the actual field testing, if you will."

"So that's where they take the prisoners?"

"Exactly."

"So, if we were to publicize one spot, *that* would be the one."

"Exactly. I doubt any publicity of the Arsenal would do much good because there's a pretty tight cover story there. They've been doing chemical weapons research for years. It's no mystery. The other facility is the one…"

His voice suddenly stopped as his body lurched forward. He fell towards Billy, nearly knocking him over. As Billy bent to help Nate to the ground, a bullet hissed near his left ear. Somebody was shooting at him from across the river. Billy turned immediately, ran back towards the street, and ducked behind a railing.

The next bullet ricocheted loudly off the metal railing only inches from Billy's head, and the people in the Market scattered. Billy ran to his truck.

He approached his truck as another bullet struck the hood. It seemed to be coming from the same firing location, but he still heard no gunshots. He got into the truck, started the engine, and drove over the curb forward to get back onto the street. The truck bounced hard over the curb but the elevated suspension managed well. He turned southward away from the river, putting additional distance between himself and the shooter. Another bullet slammed into the rear quarter panel of the truck as he sped away.

He looked intently in his rear-view mirror to see if he was being followed and saw a blue sedan pull onto the street behind him. He drove faster and made a violent turn back to the left on a side street but saw no trailers in his rear-view mirror. Relieved, he made his way further south to the interstate highway and headed west.

He imagined that whoever killed Nate now knew what he looked like and what he was driving, so he knew that he needed to change vehicles. He drove back into West Little Rock and parked in the large lot of a Home Depot store, across from a car dealership. He abandoned the truck there, knowing it likely would sit undiscovered for days.

He emptied out the truck, packing all of his belongings into his backpack and walked to the GMC dealership where a small maroon GMC Jimmy caught his eye. He offered seven thousand dollars cash for it, which they took; but, he was almost out of cash. He then drove north out of town, heading back to the cabin.

- twenty two -

Cabin fever had definitely set in for both Jules and Joe. After six straight days, they were weary of each other's company. Jules was very concerned about what her co-workers thought since the Federal agents took her out of the studio. She was accused of being at least an accomplice in an assault on Federal agents. Gone for nearly a week, she would be presumed guilty, she thought.

After many years of hard work to build her reputation, to have it taken away in a single day was devastating. She felt strongly that she needed to make contact with someone back at her station, at least to let them know that she was okay. She could tell them that whatever the accusations were, she was innocent. Peter, the station manager, had always been a good friend, someone that Jules felt she could trust.

Joe had gone to bed early, and Jules sat in the living room watching television, somewhat entertained by her fourth episode of *Law and Order* that day, and thought again about calling back to her station. She stood up from the couch and walked quietly out the front door, debating the decision to use her cell phone to call. She was sure that she would have to keep her call short—a call less than two or three minutes will be fine, she thought.

She turned on her cell phone for the first time in six days. After a few seconds, she had good signal strength. She dialed the direct line to her manager's office, knowing he would be available because the ten o'clock news was about to go to air. After three rings, she felt reassured by the voice on the other end.

"This is Peter." The voice was strong.

"Peter?"

Tears welled up in her eyes as she spoke.

"Jules? Is that you?"

"Yeah. I'm sorry for crying, but you have no idea how good it is to hear a friendly voice," Jules said with more strength.

"Jules, where are you? We've been worried. They're saying some pretty amazing things."

"I'm safe. And I've done nothing wrong. I need you to understand that, more than anything right now. All of what you've heard is a lie."

"Who are you with, Jules?"

"I'm with Dr. Mason. I can't tell you the details right now, but you must understand that there's a lot of stuff going on that's not what it seems. We're in the middle of an incredibly big story. The people we're fighting will stop at nothing to prevent this story from becoming public, and I'll tell you it goes to the highest levels of our government."

"Slow down, Jules, slow down. What you're saying doesn't make any sense to me."

"I know. I can't talk right now because they're watching, but I promise I'll be back soon, and I'll bring the biggest story of our lives."

"Jules, where are you? Why don't you let me send some help to you? Let me help."

"I'm sorry, Peter...listen. Tell everyone I'm okay."

"Take care of yourself. You call me if I can help in any way. You know we're here for you."

"I know...thanks."

Jules closed the cell phone and stood outside staring up at the sky. It was a clear night, but still quite warm. She was reassured by the sound of a familiar voice.

◆ ◆ ◆

Peter was stunned that she had called him. With all the pressure on her, he was surprised that she would call anyone. He knew that she had no family and that her work was her life, but he was still surprised that she had called. After his meeting two nights ago, he knew the truth, but it still surprised him. He picked up the phone and dialed.

After several rings, "Hello?"

"Well, it happened just like you thought," Peter said.

"Peter?"

"Yeah, it's me. I can't believe it. I just got off the phone with Jules. She said she's with the doctor as well."

Dr. Bradley sat up quickly.

"Where are they? Did she say where they are?"

"No, she just wanted to call me to say she was okay."

"How long did you talk?"

"Oh, only a couple of minutes. I'll tell you, she's about as hard-nosed a woman as I've seen in this business in twenty-five years, and she sounded pretty shook up."

"I'll track it down. We should be able to get her located pretty well. As I promised you before, we'll take care of her."

"Doc, you also promised to keep us first in line with any release of information. I've kept my promise, and I expect you'll keep yours."

"I will, Peter, I will. Thanks for calling, good night."

"Good-night, Dr. Bradley."

♦ ♦ ♦

Finally, Mercury thought, a break in the intelligence. Her cell phone had been turned on thirty minutes ago as she made a short call back to Little Rock. This made locating her fairly easy. He took her cell phone ID number listed among the intelligence reports and tapped into the NSA database for cell location.

He loaded the cell tower GPS locations and the relative signal strengths for three of the towers that detected the cell phone signal. He then put the numbers into a spreadsheet to do the mathematics, calculating the precise latitude and longitude of the cell phone signal.

He then uploaded satellite photo data from the Internet for the exact coordinates. It looked like the signal came from just outside a small structure located near the town of Jasper, in the mountains of northern Arkansas.

The remote location would make his job easier, he thought, but it would take over two hours by car to get there. He couldn't get a helicopter quickly enough to save time, so he packed up his computer and walked towards his car for the long drive.

His car was fully loaded and ready to go in anticipation of this moment. He placed his computer gear in the passenger seat and pulled out into traffic south on Main Street in downtown Little Rock, frustrated by the traffic lights, which slowed his progress.

He estimated the government's response time to the situational change. The FBI would take about an hour to process the information regarding her cell phone. They would then take about an hour to get the necessary court order for the house; they would then assemble the local and county officers to coordinate the arrest. Likely, they would send the local officers to monitor the house to ensure that if the subjects left the property, they could be tracked.

This delay should give him enough time to find his target and complete the contract. He hoped for a relatively short turnaround time for the trip, and then he could fly back home to Switzerland the following morning.

♦　♦　♦

Billy was pleased with his new purchase, a maroon 2000-model GMC Jimmy. It drove smoothly across the rough pavement on the interstate highway. He stopped briefly in Russellville, Arkansas, to get a bite to eat and a milkshake to keep him company on the road north to the cabin. He was looking forward to getting back home; he was both physically and mentally exhausted.

He had gathered a good amount of information that should help them to open up the case. He was pleased with the progress but was still disturbed by the shooting. Who had killed Nate, and how did they know about the meeting? Nate said in their first meeting that there was dissension within the government about the Project and its execution. It seemed most likely that the dissension included espionage and war against each other. What a waste of resources, he thought.

Construction work along the last few miles before Jasper slowed his progress. He thought he would arrive by eight o'clock, just before sunset.

◆ ◆ ◆

Mercury arrived in Jasper just as the sun was setting over the ridge that overlooked the western end of town. He drove north into town and was surprised at how many abandoned buildings flanked the street on both sides.

He had marked the GPS coordinates of the site of the cell phone call on his computer map, which showed that it originated about a mile out of town on Highway 74. He approached signs for the highway junction and saw a small abandoned gas station nearby, so he pulled around the rear of the building to prepare.

Once stopped, he got out of the car and walked around to the back. He opened the trunk where had stored his necessary tools: a Glock Model 19(C) compact handgun and an Austrian-made Steyr SSG-SD sniper rifle with a custom stock. He found these two guns covered nearly all situations, with the exception of jobs that required a large caliber weapon, such as shooting through walls to hit his target. For such heavy jobs, he favored the Steyr IWS 2000 that fired 15.2mm armor piercing rounds. It provided enough firepower even to bring down small aircraft. Unfortunately, jobs that required such heavy equipment had to be managed differently. For this job, he was able to use his standard methods.

Transporting firearms or explosives into the United States was more difficult. He never carried such equipment with him when he traveled by air. Instead, once he knew his target, he shipped his gear by standard FedEx. He disassembled the weapons and sent the components to separate FedEx stores where the staff held the shipments in a secure location for convenient pick-up. The great irony, he thought, is that as the airline security tightened, shipping security loosened.

In the trunk, he had his typical pack in place including a preloaded shoulder holster with the Glock handgun on the left shoulder mount and four clips holding fifteen rounds each. This will be a small job, he thought, and sixty rounds should be plenty. He knew that local officers were likely watching the area, so he took out the sniper rifle and placed it in the front seat. Once ready, he drove back out onto the road, heading west towards the GPS coordinates.

Close to the target, he noticed two police sedans parked along the highway. He turned to the right, off of the highway, into a small dirt driveway. The area appeared quiet, and the dense brush served as excellent cover. He lifted the rifle out of the front seat and left the car. He noticed that the trees overhead were fairly dense, a combination of oak and pine trees. Because of the thick canopy, the underbrush was relatively thin and easy to move through. The brush near the road was much thicker, which was perfect for concealment, especially in the low light of dusk.

As he moved quietly through the trees, he saw the two police sedans ahead. He crouched in a position about a hundred yards from the targets and positioned himself prone, chest down, and peered through the rifle scope. Once his targets were sighted and distance calculated, he removed the silencer from his pack, placed it on the end of the gun and locked it into position. He peered again through the scope and planned his strategy. With the summer heat, both sedans had all windows down. He planned two sets of rapid shots for each sedan.

He lined up the crosshairs on the right temple of the first officer and pulled the trigger. The only sound from the gun was a small, dull thump as the silencer worked well. The spray of blood from the first officer's head wound startled his partner in the left front seat. He fired a second shot that entered the other officer's head just above his nose as he turned to look at his partner slumping towards him.

Mercury then took aim at the second sedan, which was parked in front of the first. Again, in less than three seconds, he fired two shots with lethal accuracy. He waited about twenty seconds, scanning his surroundings for movement, and then stood up to move parallel to the road towards the final target; his GPS unit showed that it was just fifty meters ahead. He stopped short and saw a small wooden cabin.

He saw a woman sitting on a couch, so he moved slowly through the trees to get a closer look. He waited about five minutes in the trees but still saw no sign of the other targets. Perhaps, the other targets are gone, he thought. However, the information he received said that they would likely be together at all times. He thought that it was much more likely that the other targets were inside the cabin as well but just weren't yet visible. He decided to wait a few more minutes.

- twenty three -

Billy made the final turn into Jasper on Highway 7. Not far to go, he thought. As he drove up the hill, he noticed two police cars parked on the side of the road ahead. To avoid them, he turned into a driveway to the right. Off the side of the driveway was another car, a beige Chrysler 300M.

With the two police cars and the beige Chrysler, Billy thought that agents were likely closing in on the cabin. He felt he had no choice; he would walk through the woods to the house to see what was happening.

The sun was setting and the light was poor as he moved through the wooded area. He knew the area well, so he was able to move quickly, despite the approaching darkness. After a short distance, he came parallel to the police cars, which he could see through a clearing of trees on the road.

He noticed in the rear car that the windshield was red with blood and a body was slumped backward in the seat. In the front car, he saw nobody, but the driver's side window was shattered and completely red as well.

He moved silently through the woods to get closer to the cars. The underbrush became thicker and much harder to move through once he was near the road. He paused briefly to look around to see if any other cars were visible, but there weren't any. He moved out of the brush, crouching low, and approached the rear car, a squad car of the Newton County Sheriff. Billy peered over the passenger door through the window. The driver was slumped backwards facing forward with his eyes open and a single bullet wound in the forehead. The other officer was sideways with his head resting face down against the knee of his partner. The front seat was soaked, and the entire interior was stippled with blood.

Billy moved back into the brush and stood low on one knee as his mind raced. Jules and Joe weren't in danger of arrest—they were in danger of assassination.

◆　◆　◆

"Hey, Joe, do you want bread with your pasta?" Jules said as she poured some tea into a glass.

"Yeah, whatever you're having is fine," Joe said from the back room as he dried his hair fresh from the shower.

"I'm going with plain bread if that's okay."

"No problem." Joe walked back into the living room. "Wow, it gets dark quickly here."

He walked over to the side window and looked outward.

"Here we go," Jules said proudly as she set two plates on the small table. After five days of Joe's cooking, she was ready to take a turn.

"Looks great. I'm starving."

The meal was simple: boiled pasta with Prego sauce from a jar. Joe sat at the table as Jules walked to the refrigerator and opened the door.

Suddenly, the front door burst open, striking Joe in the left shoulder as he sat in the chair. As soon as the door opened, a thin, olive-skinned man with slight features and dark hair moved quickly into the room, stood over Joe and aimed a small pistol towards him. Jules jumped backward towards the sink.

"Move...move now!" the man said with a French accent, motioning with his gun for Joe to move into the living room.

Stunned, Joe stood up slowly facing the man, placing himself between the unknown man and Jules.

"What do you want?"

"Move over to the wall." He motioned again with the gun for them to move, as he scanned the room.

Joe moved very slowly. He knew that the man was there to kill them, but he also knew that he couldn't get the gun. He considered running at the man to try to save Jules, but he knew that this would be futile. He moved slowly to the left as instructed, and Jules moved with Joe across the living room.

Two loud gunshots pierced the silence. Joe instinctively lunged backward, shielding Jules. A third shot rang out with a quick flash from the man's gun. The bullet whirred past Joe's head and lodged in the wall above him. Joe's lunge knocked Jules back into the wall, and they both fell to the ground. As they looked up, the man's body fell forward with his face striking the floor.

Billy stood outside the door with his gun raised.

He ran up the steps into the living room and placed his foot on the back of the man's neck. Joe rose from the floor, crawled over to the man's body, and placed his index finger over the man's neck. He felt a faint pulse over the carotid artery, but after a few more beats, it ceased.

"He's dead."

"Who the hell was he?" Jules asked as she stood up from the floor.

Billy closed the front door behind him. "That man, I would say, was your executioner. What I can't figure out is how he found you. There's just no way he could trace you to me or to this place. He had to have some help. Did you guys ever leave?"

"No way, Billy. We've been in prison here for the last week with no contact with the outside world at all." Joe stood up and stepped away from the body. "Your phone rang once, I think it was Wednesday, but we didn't pick it up."

Jules stepped back into the kitchen with her hands clasped behind her head staring at the ceiling, silent.

Joe felt something was wrong as she walked back into the kitchen. "What did you do, Jules? What did you do?"

"I did make one short cell phone call."

"What...you did what? When...when did you call?" Joe stood up.

"I called Peter back at the station, you know, just to let him know I was...we were...okay."

"*When* did you call, Jules?" Billy asked.

Joe walked out the front door and down the steps.

"I don't know," Jules said. "Maybe three or four hours ago."

"Damn, Jules, do you know how stupid that was?"

"I thought, you know, I thought that if I didn't talk long, then it would be okay."

"No way—they can find you the second you turn that thing on. Also, you need to know that your manager, Peter, and Dr. Bradley are probably together on this whole thing."

"What?" Jules glared at Billy. "That doesn't make any sense."

"Maybe it does. Maybe it doesn't. Hey, wait."

Billy noticed that Joe had gone outside. He ran to the open door. "Joe, get back in here, right now! You can't be out here. It's not safe. I have no idea if there are more here to finish the job or if this guy's a solo."

Joe turned and slowly climbed the steps back into the cabin. Billy closed the door behind him.

"You guys need to know what else has happened," Billy said.

"You mean there's more?" Joe said.

"There's four dead cops out there in their squad cars."

"Oh my God!"

"Out on the road, the highway, I guess a few sheriff's deputies were tipped off to your location as well. I guess they were waiting for backup before coming in. But my guess is that this guy had a different idea than you two guys being arrested."

Joe slumped down on the couch. "What are we going to do?"

"We fight back." Jules walked into the living room.

"What?" Joe said.

"We fight back. We've gotta take the fight back to them. We can't just sit here and wait for them to hit us again."

"I agree," Billy said. "But, we have to get out of here first. We've gotta go. Right now. I'll catch you guys up on what I found once we're clear. Grab anything you need and can carry and let's go."

Joe looked around the room. "There's nothing I need here."

"Me neither, let's just go," Jules said.

"Fine. Stay behind me and stay quiet."

Billy opened the door and looked outside like a nervous cat scanning the landscape. He stepped out onto the front porch and quickly made his way down the steps, moving back into the woods, retracing his previous route. Jules and Joe moved with Billy, as instructed, close behind. Nobody spoke as they trekked through the trees and light underbrush. The sun had set below the horizon with only a fading orange-pink glow lighting their way.

Joe saw two cars parked along a small dirt road. He looked to his left and saw a small, dark house at the other end of the road. The underbrush became somewhat thicker as they approached the cars. Billy walked first to the beige sedan and peered into the driver's window.

"Don't get in this one. It was here when I got here. I'll bet it belongs to the guy who came after you."

Joe looked through the window. "What's in the seat there?"

"Looks like a computer," Jules said. "Walk around and get it all, and we'll take it with us. Maybe there's something that'll help us figure some of this out."

Billy moved quickly back to the Jimmy and got into the driver's seat. "Look, we don't have time to brush for fingerprints. Just grab the stuff and let's go."

He put the key into the ignition, and the engine roared to life.

A small bag was visible in the front floorboard of the beige car. Joe shoved everything from the front seat, including the laptop computer, into the bag and jumped in the back seat of the GMC Jimmy. Jules sat in the font passenger's seat. The truck lunged in reverse gear, then immediately rocketed forward, throwing rocks and dirt backward as it accelerated out of the driveway.

At the road, Billy turned right, taking them farther out of the town. Better to stay out of Jasper, he thought, if more police are coming. He knew he had to get back to Little Rock.

In the soft glow of dusk, they wound their way through the rolling terrain of northwest Arkansas. Peaceful, Joe thought. If only the people in these houses knew what is really going on.

Joe's attention shifted back to the laptop computer. As he opened the computer, the screen glowed. "Hey, this thing's still on. I guess the dude was coming back for it."

"What's on the screen?"

Jules turned towards Joe.

"It's a map, with GPS coordinates. I'll be damned. It's a map to the cabin back there."

"That makes sense," Billy said as he stared forward at the road ahead. "I'll bet he somehow intercepted your cell phone signal and triangulated it from the towers. All of the towers have known GPS coordinates. The FCC forced cell carriers to implement stuff called angle of arrival and time of arrival of any cell signal. By looking from at least two, and better, three towers, they can precisely locate the signal source. I told you, the government does this stuff to track all of us."

"You know, Billy, I never really believed any of your paranoid bullshit before, but now, I'm not so sure. Joe...open up the browser and see where he's been on the web."

After a couple of seconds, Joe looked perplexed. "It says we're offline."

"Yeah, that just means there's no network here. Just click where it says work offline."

"How do you know so much about computers?" Joe asked.

"I just do. I've always used them for work, and you get to know them. Now…click the icon that looks like a clock with an arrow."

"Got it. Ah…I see."

"You should see to the left of the screen each day. Click today."

"It's already open. Let's see…there's several places that are just numbers with dots."

"Those are Internet addresses, not names, actual addresses. We'll have to get somewhere with Internet access to see what they are. What else is there?"

"Not much…hey, wait a minute. I'll be damned."

"What?" Jules twisted over the seat to see the screen.

Joe turned the screen so Jules could see. "I'll bet he's been doing some online banking."

"Union Bank of Switzerland. Unbelievable. He's checking out his money in his Swiss bank account."

"Too bad we don't know his numbers. Wouldn't it be great to spend the money he got paid to kill us?"

Billy laughed.

"What?" Joe looked at Billy.

"There might be a way, but I need to get the computer to a friend."

"Okay, but what can he do?"

"This guy's a computer genius. Let me just say that if the account was accessed from this computer with passwords typed on this computer, I'll bet we *can* get them."

"How?" Jules said.

"More paranoid bullshit," Billy said. "Well, you've heard of spyware, right?"

"Yeah, kinda like viruses."

"Not totally. Viruses mostly do damage. Spyware collects information. One of the most common collects keystrokes. This guy I was telling you about says that about eighty percent of all computers have this stuff on them. There's a good chance that this computer's got it on there.

"Are you serious?"

"Yep, I've been telling you, they're always watching you."

Jules said, "Joe, we need to make sure we can get back into this computer. Go to the control panel under the Users icon. See the bottom, where it says 'reset administrator password'?"

"Got it. What do you want me to set it to?"

"Just leave it blank. That way there's no password."

"Done. I'll close it down so we don't waste the battery."

"Tell us what you found out this week, Billy."

"Okay, Joe, grab my computer there and open it up. I want you to hear some stuff I recorded from Dr. Bradley and a guy named Tom. They were talking about some testing."

Joe picked up the computer and turned it on. "Put in your password."

"It's okay, you do it. It's P-A-R-A-N-O-I-D," Billy said.

"Okay, open the folder 'Bradley'."

"Now open the audio file from four days ago."

"Got it."

Joe listened but couldn't hear much with the road noise. "Do you have some headphones?"

"Yeah, they're in the bag there. Jules, can you open it and grab them for Joe?"

"Sure." Jules unzipped the bag and handed the headphones to Joe.

After plugging them in, Joe listened intently for several minutes.

"Oh, shit," Joe said.

"What?" Jules turned around in her seat. "What did he say?"

"Have you heard this stuff, Billy?" Joe asked.

"Yeah, I listened to it several times, but I didn't really understand it."

"Billy, they're talking about a vaccine. And how to deliver it. They're going to inoculate the whole population against the weapon…secretly. Nobody will know."

"Oh my God. How are they going to do that? How are they going to give everyone the vaccine without the people knowing it?" Jules asked.

"I don't know. They just say that it's underway, and it'll take three weeks. I'll be damned. I still don't understand why they don't just tell people."

"Maybe there's something wrong with it," Billy said.

Joe leaned back. "I really can't believe they're actually going to do this."

"Well…at least we know what they're going to do. We just don't know how," Jules said.

"We don't really have to know how. We just need to publicize what's going on. That'll force a lot more disclosure."

"I don't know," Jules said. "We don't have much for a story yet. Not unless Billy came up with some miracles."

"I found the location of the labs…all of them, I think."

"Well, I'd say that's a good start," Joe said.

"We need an insider, Joe—somebody to tell the story. I don't think it can be us. We need somebody else to have the credibility to pull it off. We just need a bit more, I think," Jules said.

"I'll see what I can do when we get back to Little Rock," Billy said.

- twenty four -

After driving for nearly three hours, Joe, Jules, and Billy arrived in Little Rock. It was dark and had begun to rain. The interstate highway glowed with the varied colors of the city lights. Billy exited and pulled into the driveway of a Hampton Inn. Jules had swapped seats with Joe and was asleep in the back seat.

"Wait here, and I'll get a room," Billy said as he fumbled in the center console for his wallet.

"Do you want me to come in with you?" Joe asked.

"No, you guys still need to stay completely out of sight. Once they find those dead cops in Jasper, they'll be after you even more."

"What about the guy in the cabin?"

"What do you mean?"

"Won't they look into him?"

"I doubt they'll find much. The three of us probably know more about him than anyone. Once we get that computer going again, we'll know even more."

Billy got out and walked through the front door of the hotel. Joe stared out the front windshield. Beside the hotel was a Krispy Kreme doughnut shop, and the red neon lights were distorted by the raindrops on the windshield. He remembered that they usually had free wireless Internet access, so he opened up the laptop computer.

He opened the browser history again and looked at the strings of numbers. He clicked the one at the top and the browser window shifted to a Department of Homeland Security page with a password. The password window was already completed, and Joe clicked forward.

"Unbelievable," he said quietly.

He then clicked a different number. The screen changed to a text filled screen. After another automatic password, he looked at a database listing of investigation cases. The case marked 'Arkansas' captured his eye. He clicked the folder, opening it to a full listing of investigative material listed by odd-looking numbers. He clicked at random and opened one of the numbered folders. Inside were several documents, some pictures, and some audio files.

This guy has access to the main FBI and CIA database, Joe thought.

He opened one of the picture files. It was a picture of Jules, but she looked much younger.

"What are you looking at?" Jules's voice startled Joe.

"You scared me. I thought you were sleeping."

"I was. What's that? Why is my college picture on the screen?"

"The Krispy Kreme over there has a wireless Internet set-up." Joe motioned with his head towards the glowing shop. "I thought I'd see what other places this computer's been to. This is the CIA database. I was just at the Homeland Security database. The guy they sent to kill us hacked into their databases. The passwords were set up as an automatic from this computer. I just clicked and poof, here it is."

"Why do they have my college picture?"

"They probably have everything in the world about us. Billy's right, you know. They've got way too much information."

They both stared at the soft glow of the computer screen and said nothing.

Billy came out of the hotel lobby and got back into the car. "Hey, Jules, you awake now?" He looked over at Joe, "what's on the secret computer?"

"Oh, nothing much. Just the CIA mainframe and the Homeland Security main database. Just anything you ever wanted to know about anyone and more."

"Damn. I knew it," Billy said. "I told you guys they had all of this stuff."

"You're right, Billy. You're right." Joe closed the computer. "Hey, we need to go get a power cord for the computer so we don't lose the battery. You still need to get this to your friend so we can see if he can get us some passwords."

Billy started the engine. "I'll get you two to the room. Then I'll take the computer to him."

He drove out from beneath the canopy into the rain.

"The room's around back. I told the clerk that I wanted to be away from the street, so we got a back room."

Jules spoke up from the back. "Hey, I want to go with you to meet your geek friend."

"No problem, but I don't want this to be a field trip. This guy's more paranoid than I am."

Joe yawned. "Look, guys. I'll stay back in the room. I'm beat. I just want to rest."

Billy handed him a plastic card. "Here's a key. We're in room 213. I'll let you off, and then we'll take the computer."

Once around the side of the building, Joe got out of the truck as Jules moved from the backseat to the front seat by climbing over the console.

"Ya'll come back safe." Joe said.

"Sure thing, Joe. Get some rest. You look bad," Jules said.

They turned around and drove away. The rain was light and the air cooler. Joe stood outside and looked toward the sky as the cool rain hit his face. After a few seconds, he walked into the side door of the hotel and found the room. Sleep was close behind.

The soft rattle on the door awoke Joe, and he sat up quickly in the darkness. Shadows of people outside interrupted the only light source into the room from under the door. He jumped off the bed and looked to grab anything as a weapon. The door opened wide. It was Billy and Jules.

"Damn, you guys gave me a start." Joe's heart was pounding.

"You wanna tell him?" Billy asked as he looked at Jules.

"No, you go ahead," Jules said.

"Tell me what," Joe said. "What time is it?"

He glanced at the clock.

"Oh, it's about 2:30. We finally caught a break." Billy said as he closed the door behind him.

Jules turned on the light.

Billy took Joe's right arm. "Sit down. You're gonna need to sit down for this one."

"What kind of bullsh—"

Billy interrupted. "We found all kinds of stuff on that computer. Most of it we couldn't make shit from, but some of it we could."

"Like what…?"

"Like, we got all the account numbers from the bank accounts. There were actually four accounts."

"What's in them?"

Billy looked at Jules. She smiled.

"What's in them?" Joe repeated.

"Forty one million dollars."

"What?"

"Forty one million two hundred seventy-five thousand dollars to be more exact."

Jules sat next to Joe and put her arm around him. He sat motionless.

"This is ours," she said. "It's untraceable and it's ours."

Joe looked at Jules and smiled.

"So what you're telling me...is that we're gonna get to spend our own blood money."

"That's exactly what we're saying." Billy sat on the bed next to Joe. "Some of this money was just deposited. I guess that was the payment to kill us."

"We contacted the bank about the account. We then set up different accounts and moved the money. Our computer genius took a fourth for his effort and we all have a fourth, which comes out to just over ten million dollars each," Jules said.

"Here's your account number." She handed him a small slip of paper with a fourteen digit number on it with the label Union Bank of Switzerland. "You can change the password. We set your initial password to Billy's favorite. P-A-R-A-N-O-I-D."

Billy stood up and walked over to the window. He pulled back the curtains to look outside.

"We're gonna have to decide what to do from here."

"It's a tougher thing, now." Jules said. "Blowing this thing up in public exposes us to a lot of risk. With this money, we can buy new identities and move on. Billy says he knows some people who can take care of this for us."

"You want to just tuck tail and run? What about the people who are going to be killed by this Project?"

"Yeah, but ya know," Billy said as he walked away from the window, "from what I've seen of all this, it sounds like the Project will save some lives. Jules and I were talking…"

"Oh, shut up." Joe stood up. "I can't believe what I'm hearing. You guys smell money, and you lose your stomach. You forget what this is all about. It's not as much about us…"

Jules interrupted. "We just need to be practical here. I talked to Billy about what he found. It's all pretty weak. I'm not sure that it's enough to report. I've reported on stuff like this for years, and I'm telling you, we don't have much to go on."

"I don't care, Jules, we need to find a way."

"We don't have a way. You need to know that. We don't have enough."

Joe sat in the chair beside the window.

"Hey, you guys can do what you want, but I'm not quitting."

Billy and Jules looked at each other.

"Billy? You ever play poker?"

"Yeah." Billy paused as he pondered. "I think I know where you're going, and I think you're crazy."

"You can't be serious," Jules said. "They'll kill you."

"Look, I just need some help to make contact and that's it. I think I can do the rest."

"I still say you're crazy, but I like your spirit," Billy said.

Joe stood up from the chair and turned to the window, scratching his head. "Yeah, we need to get new IDs, no question. We need passports, the whole deal. Can you get that for us, Billy?"

"Sure, I can have them in forty-eight hours."

"And these people you know are good?" Jules asked.

"Hey, the papers and passports will be originals. They'll actually be government issue. It'll be flawless, guys."

"The Project people and government people don't know you, Billy," Joe said. "You're still an unknown. They know you exist, but I doubt they have anything… right?"

"I suppose so. Yeah, I'm pretty clean, I guess."

"Jules and I need to leave. And with all of what's going on, you may want to leave. I don't want to be around if the bug is released by terrorists or the government forces a mostly untested vaccine on the public. I just don't want to be here when it all goes down."

"I've got nowhere to go here anyway," Jules agreed. "I like the idea of leaving for a while. I wouldn't know where to go, though."

"I know where to go…someplace away but still civilized. I've read about the place in a book. I've wanted to go there a long time anyway. It's perfect."

"Where is it?" Billy asked.

"I'm going to keep it secret until we're gone. I just don't want anything to interfere. The less you know about where we're going, the better."

"You're right," Billy agreed. "We just need to get you guys some new IDs. You need to officially cease to exist."

"Listen, Jules. As soon as possible you need to leave here. We'll get you somewhere safe for a while. I want you to get a new cell phone with your new ID, prepaid, you know, something fairly anonymous. When I'm done with what I have to do, I'll call you and tell you what I've arranged. I'll set you up to travel starting from a small airport so that security checks will be lower tech, no face recognition or stuff like that. We can change our outward appearance, but we have to be careful. Jules, I know you've loved being a blonde, but…"

Billy laughed.

"What are you laughing at?" she said.

"Nothing…I just can't picture you as anything but a blonde," Billy said.

"Billy, we need you to go to the store and get some hair color for Jules."

Billy continued laughing.

"While you're out," Jules interrupted, "get Joe some peroxide. If I'm going from blonde to brunette, then Joe is going from brunette to a blonde. And get some clippers. He's going short, too."

"Short's a good idea," said Joe. "We'll cut yours in half, go about shoulder length."

"Anything else, you know, while I'm out."

"Yeah," Jules said. "If I'm screwing with my looks, I'm going to need several beers."

"Done. I'll grab some food, too."

Billy walked to the door.

"Where are we going, Joe?" said Jules.

"I'll tell you when we're safely on the plane."

"How am I going to know what plane to be on?"

"I'll take care of it."

Joe walked into the small bathroom and splashed some water on his face.

"And, Billy, I'm going to need to pack an extra bag, before we go, just in case something goes wrong."

"I know what you mean," Billy replied. "I can definitely help with that."

"Jules, you told me that you worked with a guy in Dallas who is now a producer for ABC, right?"

"Yeah, what are thinking?"

"I think you need to deliver him the story of his career. We can give him the biggest pieces and let him report it. We can tell him everything—about the threat, the Project, and the vaccine. The public deserves to know the truth. Let them choose if they want the vaccine or not."

"I'll take care of it, but you know that once this is done, you'll have nothing left to bargain with. If something happens to you, they'll bury you," Jules said.

"I understand. I think I can do this, but above all else, people need to know what's going on. Can you please promise me you'll do that?"

"I promise. I'll take care of it," Jules said as she hugged Joe.

- twenty five -

"You look exhausted."

"Thanks for noticing, Mildred," Dr. Bradley said as he closed his office door. "This back and forth travel is killing me. I think I haven't had a day off in a month."

"Actually," Mildred shuffled her papers, "it's been twenty-six days."

Dr. Bradley walked to the double doors of the Medicine Department Office at the VA Hospital. "Do you need anything else from me?"

"No, sir. Go home to Barbara. Get something to eat, and get some rest."

"Thanks."

"You're welcome, sir."

Dr. Bradley walked down the hall toward the elevators. He was still bothered by the necessity of ordering Viper to eliminate Joe and the reporter, but it was necessary for the survival and eventual success of the Project.

"Sad," he murmured under his breath.

Even though the sun was almost completely set, it was still uncomfortably hot as he walked into the parking garage. As he glanced back to open his door, he was thrust forward into the side of the car, pinned from behind.

"How does it feel to be touched by a dead man?"

"Joe?…oh my God…is that you?" Dr. Bradley said.

"No, it's the ghost of Joe. Because you had me killed."

"Oh my God…"

Joe slapped the back of Dr. Bradley's head.

"You no-good son-of-a-bitch."

"Joe, I'm so sorry. You don't understand the pressure I'm under…"

"Don't even try that."

"But I had no choice…"

"Shut up. Not another word out of you, or I'll kill you right here. I don't care. You need to listen, and I promise you need to listen good. Don't tell me 'I had no choice'. That's bullshit, and you know it. We *always* have choices. Get in the car."

Joe shoved him into the driver's seat as he opened the rear door behind Dr. Bradley and sat in the back seat.

Billy observed the situation in front of him. He had driven Joe to the car and agreed to follow them until Joe finished with Dr. Bradley.

"Joe, I…"

"I said shut up!" Joe slapped the back of Dr. Bradley's head again, harder. "Drive, dammit."

"Where am I going?"

"Go east on I-630, and I'll tell you where to turn. Just drive."

As ordered, Dr. Bradley backed out of his reserved parking space and exited the garage. He drove to the interstate onramp and merged into traffic.

"What do you want, Joe?"

"Since you follow orders so well, I'm going to start with a few of my own. You have to understand that I have a lot more power now than you think because I *am* alive and I will not stop until the Project is wide open. So as God is my witness, you, or your President, need to open it all up and explain it to America. Explain to them why it's absolutely necessary. Explain to the families of the prisoners why they have to die—miserably."

Dr. Bradley continued driving, staring forward, listening to Joe.

"I have a proposal for you and your President. We know almost everything about your Project. We know what you're doing at Cummins prison. We know what you're doing at the

Pine Bluff Arsenal. We know what you're doing in that warehouse building south of Pine Bluff, and we have pictures."

"Damn it," Dr. Bradley muttered.

"We have videotape of you in all these places. We've tracked your every move. All of this information combined with *my* story will be bigger than Watergate. But you and your President can avoid all of this if you just do it on your own. I'll grant you that opportunity."

"You have no idea what you've done..."

"Like hell, I don't know," Joe interrupted. "I know more than you think."

Billy looked in his rear-view mirror in horror as three black Chevy Suburbans were speeding forward. He knew the situation wasn't recoverable and felt helpless that he couldn't warn Joe, nor could he do anything to prevent what he knew was about to happen.

"No, Joe, you don't know what you're doing, or you wouldn't be here right now," Dr. Bradley said.

The black Suburbans surrounded Dr. Bradley's car on both sides. He slowed as a third Suburban approached the rear. Joe looked around the car.

"You really have no idea what you've done. You should have remained in the dark."

He slowed the car to a stop in the middle of the roadway. As they stopped, four men dressed in dark suits and armed with automatic weapons opened the car and ripped Joe from the back seat and forced him face down on the searing pavement. They placed cuffs on his wrists behind his back and jerked him into the back seat of a Suburban. Within about thirty seconds, Joe had moved from one back seat to the other.

They drove eastward on I-630. Nobody spoke; the men on either side of him stared straight ahead out the front windshield. Joe knew the futility of trying to escape. The Suburbans turned south on I-30 and then east again on I-440. After about ten minutes, they exited the road. Joe's heart sank again—they were going to the airport.

The trucks turned off the main road towards general aviation and drove directly to the tarmac. A white jet waited with engines running. The trucks pulled up to the side of the plane as the door opened extending the ladder downward to the tarmac. The men in suits forced Joe from the Suburban and directed him up the ladder and down into the left front seat. Two of the men followed behind into the airplane and closed the cabin door behind them. Without speaking, one of the men removed the handcuffs from Joe's wrists. They fastened him into the seats as the jet moved down the runway. Within two minutes, the jet was airborne and Joe was gone.

From a distance, Billy watched helplessly as the white jet disappeared into the clouds. Joe warned him that if anything happened to him to take Jules away. They had discussed an alternative plan, just in case. He had forty-eight hours; if Joe didn't contact him in forty-eight hours, he knew what to do.

- twenty six -

Joe could barely believe his eyes. When they had removed him from Dr. Bradley's car, he had assumed that he would be taken out to a remote location and dispatched efficiently where nobody would find the body. Instead, after a two-hour flight, he was bundled into a van. The van drove through immense iron gates and up a paved semi-circle drive.

The tall man accompanying Joe escorted him under the portico at the west end of the building, then down a short hallway into a small lobby. He had never been here before, but he recognized many of the sights. After waiting about fifteen minutes in a comfortable chair, he was escorted down another short hallway, turned to the right, and ushered into perhaps the most recognizable room in the world—the Oval Office. Behind the large ornately carved wooden desk sat the

President of the United States. She was completing a phone call.

She's smaller in person, Joe thought; she seems much taller when she is on television. Yet she still had an air of importance surrounding her and seemed quite at ease with her position behind the desk. Joe stood, as instructed, in front of the desk. As soon as she hung up the receiver, she stood up and walked around the desk towards Joe.

"Dr. Mason, it's good to meet you in person," she said as she extended her hand.

Joe returned the uncomfortable handshake.

"Nice to meet you, Madam President."

"I'm deeply sorry that we have to meet this way. There are many days that I dislike this job very much."

She motioned for Joe to sit on one of the two couches that faced each other.

Joe sat on the edge of the couch in front of the President.

"I can't imagine what you think of me and my Administration."

"Frankly, it's not positive, ma'am," Joe said.

"Many things happen in my Administration without my direct knowledge and supervision. I set broad policy from that desk and from this office. But I'm unable to make every single decision personally and supervise every action taken on behalf of this Administration. I have to delegate."

"I understand."

"Did you know that I have a daughter, near your age?

"Yes, ma'am. I think so, ma'am."

"You understand that a mother views the world very differently from anyone else, don't you?"

"Yes, ma'am. I think so."

"Did you know that many people think it's a weakness for someone in a position of power—an Achilles heel?"

"No, ma'am. I don't think I ever thought of it that way."

"Well, let me tell you, after eighteen years in Washington, which should more than qualify me, many people still are uncomfortable with a woman sitting behind that desk."

"Yes, ma'am. I see your point."

"Many people still attempt to shield certain hard facts from me, thinking, I guess, if I'm faced with hard choices, the motherly side of me may limit me from doing the right thing. Do you understand how that can happen?"

"Yes, ma'am, quite clearly."

"Do you understand how that can happen when somebody orders the killing of a private, productive American citizen because they *know too much* and leave the motherly President out of the decision?"

"Yes, ma'am."

"Here's where I have the hardest, most difficult job in the world. In our own Declaration of Independence, we declared both life and liberty as inalienable rights. Do you remember that?"

"Yes, ma'am."

"I ask the hardest question of all: what happens when there's absolutely no way you can have both life *and* liberty? What do you do then? Which do you protect? Which do you sacrifice? I think it's the most difficult question in government. Our government isn't unique in struggling to answer this most basic dilemma. Are you still following me, Dr. Mason?

"Yes, ma'am."

"I cannot possibly know what the last few weeks have been like for you." The President touched Joe's hand as she leaned forward. "It'll take time for the power base here to accept a woman behind that desk. It'll also take time for the decisions that come from behind that desk to retain some character of a woman's perspective. I happen to think it's long overdue, Dr. Mason."

"Yes, ma'am, on that point, I think you're very right."

She leaned back.

"Now, I've had full knowledge of certain parts of this Project, such as what's been required of prisoners. However, your involvement and the details of your subsequent problems were not revealed to me. Two people on my staff, who have already worked their last day, were afraid of what I'd do if I knew the details about Dr. Joe Mason, Ms. Jules Green, and Dr. Brad Yates. You need to understand that I will do anything I can to protect this Project. I strongly believe it's my duty to protect the American people. We cannot have public knowledge of the Project, not right now. The American people cannot possibly comprehend the situation well enough to make good decisions. Fear cripples people at times like this. Can you understand that?"

"Yes, ma'am, quite clearly."

"So I will stand by the Project and its completion, and I simply cannot see how anyone will be well-served by having a media frenzy about it. Not right now. As I said before, many times before, and I will say again, history will judge me. But I need you to leave all of this alone. That's why I've brought you here today, and that's exactly what I would have personally asked you to do earlier, if I'd been given the chance. These types of requests are best made directly and personally. I know that I'm asking you to do something that you may not feel is right. But I'm asking anyway. We've already started the public vaccination program, but it will take time. Any early publicity will invite an immediate attack. You understand that, don't you?"

"I understand, ma'am. But it's very hard for me to accept that I'll be allowed to walk out of here tonight and see more than one more tomorrow, no matter what I tell you right now."

Joe trembled as he spoke.

"I can see your point," the President said. "You do have insurance, however. You have insurance that protects you even now."

"I'm not clear how I have anything of the sort."

"You have a mystery man on your side."

Joe smiled as he began to follow her.

"You have a man on your side that we simply cannot identify or locate. No matter how hard we've tried and believe me, we've tried, we simply don't know who he is. I've informed everyone that you are absolutely off limits for now.

I've explained to those people that still want you eliminated that even if they were to succeed, the mystery man still exists. I've made it clear that eliminating you or Ms. Green at this time serves no purpose—it does *not* help this Administration."

"I follow you, ma'am."

"I'm a political veteran, Dr. Mason. You don't get to sit behind that desk without political scars and balancing acts. I'm going to advise you on two points, if you don't mind."

"I'm listening."

"You need to disappear for a long time, number one, and number two, you need to ensure above all else that your mystery man remains a mystery."

"I understand, ma'am. I'm covered."

The President stood up from the couch, and Joe stood in response.

"Dr. Mason, you know it's going to be a really bad flu year. My HHS Secretary tells me that the Avian flu may push through this year."

"Yes, ma'am. I've heard. Your aggressive approach is good, I think. You've done a good thing in offering the vaccine and a booster for free," Joe said with a polite smile.

"Make sure you get your flu shot, Dr. Mason. *Especially this year.*"

Joe glared back at her. He understood.

She turned to walk towards the door, placing her right hand on Joe's back.

"I've instructed the men who brought you here to assist you, including flying you to anywhere you wish. Please watch yourself. And understand that all of this will be brought to the public, but I need to do it myself, in my way."

"Thank you, Madam President."

"Thank you, Dr. Mason, and take care of yourself."

The secretary looked up at Joe as the President led him out of the Oval Office into the small reception area. The tall man that brought Joe to the White House escorted him back outside.

Joe's mind raced, attempting to consider all of the changes.

He remembered his original plan.

- twenty seven -

After the congestion at the ticket counter, the line of
people at the TSA security checkpoint extended to the main
doors. Two men escorted Joe around the line to the
checkpoint.

"He's with us. We're taking him to Dallas," the agent
said to the TSA guard.

"Fine, just go to the left over there to get through."

He signaled to a woman sitting down to come over and
help.

"Take these men through the end down there."

"Thanks," the agent said.

Joe placed all of his pocket contents into the tray and
walked through the metal detector. After passing through
security himself, the agents waited for Joe.

Once on the other side, they walked down the wide
hallway. Dulles airport looked newer than Joe expected, with

glass from floor to ceiling on the sides allowing full view of the tarmac where lines of commercial planes parked. The high saddle-shaped roof provided an expansive feel on the inside as they walked down the long hallway that terminated into Concourse B. The agents stopped at the start of the concourse.

"This is as far as we go. The President asked us to stay here until you board your plane?"

"Thanks for your help." Joe extended his hand.

The agent took his hand to shake. "Take care of yourself Dr. Mason. We'll stand over there at the wall to make sure you get off okay."

"Thanks."

Joe turned and walked down the Concourse to Gate B21.

After a brief search, he found computer station and opened the web browser to send a text message. He typed the number and checked it twice to make sure. He had only one shot at this. He typed the text exactly:

```
AA Fl 1337 IAD to DFW Arr 20:30 today. Plan
meet 21:00 Gate B6. Need Pack. Follow Plan
exactly.
```

He checked the message again and then sent it.

After sending the message, he logged on to the Expedia account that he had set up before leaving Little Rock and finalized the new travel arrangements.

He stood up from the computer, walked across the tile floor towards the windows, and sat down in the chairs near the gate, looking back at the agents still standing against the wall. He knew why they remained; they were monitoring him, as they would on the plane and then off the plane when he arrived in Dallas. The difficulty, he knew, was what to do from there.

The plan will work, he thought.

He just didn't expect it to be this way. He knew that Billy had seen him dragged from Dr. Bradley's car; and after receiving the text message, Billy would know that Joe was still alive and the plan was still active.

The American Airlines gate attendant announced the final boarding call. Joe took his place in the line to board the plane. As he approached the jet bridge, he looked back to the agents. They stood still, watching him board the plane.

Joe slept during the majority of the flight. He awoke briefly as turbulence bounced the Boeing 757, rubbed his eyes, and looked slowly around the cabin of the plane. Nobody appeared to notice him, or to care, but he felt sure that someone was there.

The plan will work, he thought.

The approach to DFW was somewhat bumpy. The plane set wheels down softly on the runway and slowed to a comfortable taxi speed. Joe looked at his watch—8:23—seven minutes early. After a long taxi time, the plane arrived at the gate.

"Come on, let's go," he said quietly to himself.

Joe looked forward in the aisle, which was blocked by an obese, sweaty man in a tweed sport coat. The man struggled with his overstuffed bag and finally was able to free it from the confines of the overhead storage. As he brought it down, it thumped the top of an older lady's head. She said nothing but glared. Finally, the line began to move again. Joe walked up the narrow aisle to deplane, with no bags.

"Thanks, buh, bye," said the black-haired flight attendant in a friendly but artificial manner.

She repeated the exact phrase multiple times as Joe stepped off the plane into the jet bridge. He heard her voice echoing the same phrase as he walked.

The jet bridge emptied the passengers of the flight into Terminal B at DFW airport. Joe looked up at the ceiling and read, 'Gate B32'. He looked down at his watch—8:43

Perfect.

He walked out a few yards into the main foot traffic flow and turned right to walk the long left turning semicircle of Terminal B from gate B32 to gate B6 as planned. He recognized nobody, but he knew he was being followed.

The plan is perfect, he thought again.

His stomach growled in protest as he passed an airport restaurant without stopping. He looked at his watch again—8:49.

He passed the last TSA checkpoint on his left and was glad he was already in the secured area and so didn't have to pass through again. He looked to his right as he passed the checkpoint, to avoid face contact. As he looked, a man in a dark suit stood leaning against the wall appearing to read a newspaper, but the clear, coiled plastic earpiece caught Joe's eye. His stomach growled again but not from hunger this time.

He could see gate B6. To the left was the men's room, and Joe walked towards it. An intermittent stream of men passed through the doorway, in and out, some carrying bags, others not. Once inside, Joe quickly turned to the left towards the bank of doors leading to the toilets opposite the wall of urinals. In the middle of a series of three vacant stalls, he went inside and locked the door. To his right, he heard the lock slide closed.

A black duffle bag appeared from underneath the stall wall from the right. Joe stared at the bag and smiled. The lock to the right opened, and Joe heard footsteps walk away. He stared down again at the bag. After a brief pause and two deep breaths, he unzipped the bag.

Exactly as I packed it, he thought.

He quickly changed completely, including a Boston Red Sox baseball cap and an artificial moustache. This one had to be perfect, and it was. He packed the remainders of his own clothes into the black duffle bag and left the toilet stall. He walked around the wall and stood in front of a sink, staring at the reflection in the mirror.

Perfect, he thought, *absolutely unrecognizable*.

He washed his hands, then stared back into the mirror and took a deep breath. His heart pounded in his chest.

He walked out the doorway, blending into traffic. He kept his eyes down on a magazine as he exited the men's restroom, back to the right, back towards the direction he had come earlier.

As he walked, his heart continued to pound; his breathing was short and quick. As he walked further, now past Gate B12, he became more comfortable.

Not much farther, he thought.

He didn't look up, keeping his face glued to the magazine as he walked. After what seemed an unending time, he looked up and saw the sign for Gate B15.

Only one more to go.

As he approached Gate B15, his heart skipped a beat. Jules stood in front of him, now with shoulder-length brunette hair, dressed in jeans and a red T-shirt. She stared up at him and moved closer, then gently put her arms around his waist, holding tight. She cried as they hugged each other, among a mad flow of people scurrying from gate to gate to move on with their lives.

A hand touched Joe's back; startled, he turned around and saw Billy.

"Thanks for the bag. It worked perfectly," Joe said.

"Yep. You were right," Billy said.

"I didn't see anyone following me, not that I could tell."

"I followed you from where you got off the plane," Billy explained. "There were at least two men and I think actually a woman who tailed you all the way to men's room. None went inside, just as you thought. I tailed you from a distance out of the men's room. They definitely lost you. They'll start tearing this place apart here in a little while."

"You guys flew in okay from Fort Smith?"

"Yeah. No problems. Security there was easy, just like you thought."

"Damn, that was as nervous as I've ever been," Joe said. "You'd think being threatened, chased, and confronted by the President would be bad, but that was..."

Jules looked up at him. "The President..."

"That's where they took me."

"I don't understand how you knew...To see the President?"

"Not just that. But also in the damn Oval Office."

Billy laughed almost uncontrollably.

"What did she say? What did she want?" asked Jules.

"She was upset at what was happening. She said she had never been told about us, that somebody in her administration purposefully shielded the information from her. Said they thought that as a woman, she wouldn't have the balls to do it."

"Damn, you see, this is what I've been saying all along," Billy said. "The right hand has no idea what the left hand is doing. It's madness."

"I agree. But she said she would have asked us in person to stop, if she'd known, which is why they took me, once they found me."

"What else did she say?" Jules asked again.

"She said that the reason for all the secrecy, especially the secrecy about the vaccinations, was because if they told the public, they'd also tell the enemy that they had a vaccine. But since there's no way to get the whole population immunized in less than a few weeks, they'd invite an immediate attack. I guess it makes sense, but I still don't like it. I just know I don't want to stick around and be a lab rat."

"I agree," Jules said as they turned to walk slowly.

"Billy, are going with us?" Joe asked.

"No, I'm staying. As much as I don't trust the government here, I trust it even less everywhere else. I'll get a new place lined out and stay in the country, away from the hustle of cities—and away from doctors…no offense, Joe."

"The paranoia deepens," Joe said.

They walked slowly towards the end of Terminal B, where their flight to Newark departed in just ten minutes.

"Well, sorry, guys," Billy said. "I'm gonna get out of here and get a room and then head out in the morning."

"Sure thing."

"Hey, you still want me to deliver the package to your friend at ABC, right, Jules?"

"Yeah" Jules said. "You're okay with that still, aren't you, Joe?"

"I am," Joe replied. "Despite what she said, I still think the whole thing needs some sunlight for disinfection. Besides, you said yourself, your friend would take a while to independently verify everything before airing the story."

"Absolutely," Jules said.

"If the President is right, the vaccine will already be distributed," Joe said. "Assuming it works as they say, everyone will be protected. I guess the only variable is when the next attack comes. Will they have it all done in time?"

They stopped walking. Joe reached his hand out to shake hands with Billy. Billy took his hand, then pulled Joe forward for a strong hug.

"Billy, you saved my life, several times. Thanks," Joe said.

"You saved mine too. You've done a good thing here."

Jules stood on her toes to kiss Billy. They hugged as well. Billy turned and walked away through the security zone, out into the main terminal and away.

"You ready?" Joe asked.

"I'm so ready to be away from all of this."

They walked towards the gate to board the flight to Newark.

- twenty eight -

The air outside was cool and damp—more than either of them had expected. The flight took just over seven hours from Newark. They were exhausted from a combination of jet lag, sleep deprivation, and stress. With just two bags of essentials that they had organized in Newark, they were traveling light.

After clearing customs with their new identities, Jules and Joe stepped briefly outside into the August air in Edinburgh, Scotland. They quickly realized the difference from the August air in Arkansas; it was frigid by comparison but refreshing. They went back inside the airport to find a series of small shops on the top floor.

"I still can't believe you've brought me here," Jules said as she took Joe's hand going up the escalator.

"I've read about it in books and have seen pictures, but it's different than I expected—and colder, too. I think I saw a sign."

He looked around as his line of sight cleared floor level.

"Hey, there it is," Jules said, looking to the right, noting the purple sign. "Jenners. That's the one the guy said, right?"

"Yep. It's smaller than I expected."

They walked across the long landing towards the store. The cooler than expected climate forced them to buy warmer clothes, a common experience for first time travelers to Edinburgh. After a brief browse through the store, they both found fleece sweatshirts to take some of the bite out of the crisp air.

Jules led the way back down the escalator. "But we're not staying here in Edinburgh, you said?"

"Nope, our final spot is up the road a couple of hours."

"We're going farther north?"

"Yep. But I promise, it's a gem—at least what I've seen in the books."

"You sent some money and a note to somebody when we were in Newark?"

"Yeah."

"Who was it?"

"A friend from home."

"A friend?"

"Yeah...a friend who really deserves it. I sent exactly $490,000 to my friend Emad. He has some land he needs to buy."

"He must be a good friend."

"He's a really good friend…and a good man. He said that I'd understand what he was talking about when I had a family of my own. I understand now."

"You sound so serious."

"I'm sorry, Jules."

"It's okay. I was just curious."

"I'm sorry that I forgot to compliment you on your hair," Joe said.

"Oh…and your sweater, Joe. You really look local."

He had removed the fake moustache back in Dallas, but the new blonde hair and tourist sweatshirt made him nearly unrecognizable.

"We'll get proper attire when we get to Inverness."

They both laughed with some relief in their newfound anonymity. After a brief stop and short debate at the Hertz rental car counter, they secured a Mercedes ML270 for a month. The rental agent was uncomfortable in renting the luxury vehicle for a month without a reservation, but after a brief call to his manager, he completed the contract and sent Joe and Jules on their way.

They walked briskly out to the Mercedes.

"Oh, damn…" Joe said.

"What's wrong?" Jules said.

"The damn steering wheel is on the wrong side," Joe said.

"Do you want me to drive?"

"Hell no. A woman driver and the wrong side of the road. No way."

Jules rolled her eyes and opened the left side door and sat in the passenger seat.

They had planned their cover story on the plane. If asked, they would say that they were considering marriage. Before settling down, they were traveling around the world, living in different areas to experience life in other cultures. They were rich, from family money inherited on both sides. Joe had changed his name to Joe Taylor, and Jules had changed to Julie Smith but would still go by the name Jules.

The story had to be complete and also had to be believable, explaining why they were rich, but providing no real details about how they got their money; inheritance seemed appropriate and not altogether false.

The drive north across the Firth of Forth Bridge was relatively short. They drove along the highway through the small town of Perth, where they changed roads on their way to Inverness. Joe liked the idea of staying in Inverness, a small city in the Highlands of Scotland. It represented a haven to Joe, a city with a long history, unexplored to both of them, a city with little care of haughty world politics, and a city far from the reach and interest of the people who had targeted them. The Scottish Highlands could hide them well. While the climate was cool, the people and culture, they discovered, were inviting.

The ride north was quiet with very little conversation. Jules placed her hand on Joe's leg as he drove. The rolling hills reminded Joe of Arkansas, but the vegetation was much different. Scattered across the hills and valleys, the native heather glowed a golden yellow.

Jules read a guidebook she purchased in Edinburgh as they drove.

"Listen to this. Through Inverness, the river Ness flows through the center of town, emptying water from the famed Loch Ness into the Moray Firth. It serves as the center of activity in the city with shops, businesses, cathedrals, and a castle overlooking its bank. I think I'm going to like it here."

"This place will be great for us," Joe said. "We can stay here a while and see what happens."

Joe knew that they could stay in Scotland without visa problems for six months, but he planned to move on before that time to a warmer climate, assuming they remained safe. Joe also wanted to stay long enough to spend some time a short drive farther to the north in the small village of Dornoch, Scotland, home of the Royal Dornoch Golf Links. He had played several rounds in Little Rock with a retired banker who bragged about his two-week trip to Dornoch, and since that time, Joe knew he needed to go—this was his chance.

They knew their lives would never be the same. They knew that in time they might return to their native country, but they knew it would be a long time—a long time before it would be safe.

- twenty nine -

The backpack was heavier than the man expected. Fully loaded, it weighed almost fifty pounds, but it was worth the work—a small price to pay for martyrdom. The explosive primacord wrapped around the center of his chest guaranteed his body would be split into two pieces at the first detonation, but the second explosion, timed for five seconds after the first, guaranteed victory in jihad. The cargo he carried would kill thousands of infidels.

He pushed through the crowd of people trying to get on the subway train; he had only twenty minutes to get from the Grand Central-42nd Street green line station all the way down to the Broadway-Wall Street station and then walk the one block down to Broad Street to get to his target, the New York Stock Exchange.

Only twenty minutes, he thought, *barely enough time.*

The timing was important, he knew. When he got the phone call, the voice had told him that the timing needed to be perfect—the bombings had to be simultaneous for the most devastating effect. He was proud to be called to serve. He had been in New York City for almost four years, completing his degree in civil engineering at NYU. He knew that his family would mourn his death, but his father would be proud. Ever since eviction in 1947 from their home in Palestine, the family had struggled in squalor in the West Bank for the last two generations. Education was important, but all too limited by opportunity to advance. When a scholarship grant presented itself, his father encouraged him to go to the United States. Engineers would be needed, he thought, once the Israeli state was destroyed and Palestine was restored. Restoration work needed construction, and construction work required qualified engineers.

Martyrdom seemed to him a small sacrifice to help ensure victory, and this strike at the heart of the American capital market would devastate their ability to aid the Israeli state. He hadn't planned the attack. Others had done that, but he was honored to help the mission. He wasn't sure what was inside the four metal canisters on his back, but the man who delivered them was cautious when loading them it into the pack. The small plastic switch in his right hand felt larger, as he knew it controlled a great weapon, a great hope for his people.

Once inside the subway train, he stood near the door, crowded by the people around him. He noted a variety of people—a young couple sitting beside each other, the woman appeared to be pregnant, two men in dark suits each with a briefcase, one man standing and reading a newspaper with his left knee wrapping around the pole to steady himself against the lurching of the subway car as it traveled southward. To his left was an older woman with a grocery sack, and next to her was a young child with sandy blonde hair and blue eyes. The child looked at him and smiled. He smiled in reply, a bit strained. The weight of the pack dug into his back.

With each stop, people exchanged places—different faces and colors, but similar in appearance. Everyone seemed busy with their lives, too busy to concern themselves with the life and death struggle that his family faced back home.

Nobody cares, he thought. *That is why you must die.*

He remembered from the Scripture that the world is divided into two spheres, *Dar al-Islam,* the Land of the Pure, and *Dar al-Harb,* the Land of Warfare, a land belonging to infidels that hasn't been subdued by Islam. Only through jihad can *Dar al-Harb* become *Dar-al Islam.* He remembered the promise of the Scripture:

> *Let those who fight in the cause of Allah who barter the life of this world for that which is to come; for whoever fights on Allah's path, whether he is killed or triumphs, we will give him a handsome reward.*

He finally reached the Broadway-Wall Street station and made his way off the subway train. The escalators out to the city were to his left and he cinched his pack tighter as he ascended from below. The sunlight was bright, harsh on his eyes as he struggled to adjust from the darkness below; however, it warmed his face as he stopped beyond the escalator and lifted his gaze upward. He glanced down at his watch, only four minutes until salvation.

He walked with quick steps southward along Broadway among the bustle of others on their way to work, now in the heart of the financial district of Manhattan, indeed a financial center of the world. One block south, he turned left towards the target and noted the façade of the building and remembered reading somewhere that the building's front was modeled after a Roman temple.

How appropriate, he thought.

The ring of his cell phone startled him. He fumbled with the phone to answer the call, his last call.

"Hello, this is Amir," he said in English.

"Allah be with you," the voice replied in Arabic.

"And with you."

"Are you in position?"

"Yes, perfect."

"Hold the line a moment."

He waited, staring up at the limestone columns across the street. It was 10:30 a.m., and the Stock Exchange bustled with business.

"Are you still there?" a different voice asked.

"Yes."

"I have put all of you on the phone at once to give you all good news. You are all just moments away from salvation, and you are all to be praised for your bravery in jihad in the service of Allah. Before you go, I thought you should know the mission. You have served in silence, in isolation of each other, and now I bring you together. You are in New York City, in three places. You are in London, in two places. You are in Los Angeles, and you are in Sydney. These places symbolize, each in their own way, the monuments of Satan. You will serve as Allah's hand."

All of these places...fantastic!

"Allah be with you all. Go, my brothers. Go on your way," the voice said, followed by silence.

"Allahu Akbar," he said aloud to himself.

He looked up one last time to the blue sky, then looked forward at the Roman temple in front of him and pushed the plastic button in his right hand.

- thirty -

Ten days after Jules and Joe arrived, life was returning to a routine but certainly not normal. The new city opened itself for them to explore, despite what was happening in the world at large.

Since they had no other clothes when they arrived, they needed to replenish the basics: some pants, some shirts, some socks and underwear, some shoes, and, of course, an overcoat. Being more particular in her tastes, she wanted to stay longer in the clothing store. Leaving her to finish, he pushed through the brass-handled oak door into an adjacent pub. The lone bartender stood behind the bar, watching the television, and he didn't look away when Joe entered. Dark wood surrounded the bar and extended around the room as a high wainscot—pictures of various tartans dotted the wall.

"Bloody Americans...get us into the mess and then not help us. Now look at us."

Joe sat on the stool closest to the door.

"Bloody Yanks."

"Can you pour me a stout?" Joe asked, revealing his accent and his nationality.

"Of course…sorry, sir," the bartender said as he pushed a small bowl of pretzels towards Joe.

He turned around and pulled a tall glass from the shelf, never taking his eyes off the television coverage of the events in all five cities. He poured the beer slowly, correctly.

"Look at the difference. They said just a bit ago, London had over two thousand dead and Sydney had almost five thousand dead. And we're just a week into this. It's going higher, they say."

"It'll go higher," Joe said.

"New York had it easier," the bartender continued, as he set the glass on the down. "New York! They had three explosions and only thirty-three dead…just from the explosions. Only nine died later. Nine! That's not right."

"Maybe they were prepared," Joe said.

"Prepared?"

Joe remained silent and took a slow sip of the stout beer.

"Bloody Yanks."

You weren't told because you can't handle it, Joe thought.

The television reports were the only sound in the pub and had continued non-stop since the explosions. The three other patrons were silent, rapt. Joe noticed that the coverage had shifted to the futile medical treatment and the massive and growing casualty count.

"And since you know so much, Yank, what's with the reports of a vaccine?"

Joe said nothing.

"They had some report about a vaccine given. Said it was a secret."

"Yeah, I heard that, too."

"Well, I thinks it's rubbish."

"Maybe."

"It's rubbish. No way they'd hold that back. No way."

"Maybe." Joe took another slow sip.

"So, why are you here, Yank, so far from home?" the bartender said with a lighter tone.

"Traveling with a friend to get away. I've always wanted to visit."

"Are you liking it?"

"Yeah, it's slower...I like it."

"Guess you can't go home for a while. No planes worldwide for a week they're saying. Don't know when they'll fly again."

"I guess I'm stuck here for a while."

Because I didn't get the vaccine.

The bartender turned towards the door when it opened. Joe turned around as well. Jules was carrying three bags in each hand and was struggling to get through the doorway. He stood up from the stool to help her.

"Damn, did you have to buy the whole store?" He took three bags from her left hand.

"I got us fixed up for a little while—about five or six days."

"Us? What do you mean us?"

"Oh, I bought some things for you, too."

"I'm scared to look."

"It's okay, Joe. I've taken good care of you."

"That's what I'm afraid of."

Jules sat at a table away from the bar. The bartender walked around and set a small napkin on the table in front of her.

"Can I get you a drink, miss?"

"Whatever he's having is fine."

"Guinness it is, then. Be right back."

Joe sat down at the small rustic wood table across from Jules and peered into the bags.

"I don't see anything too offensive."

"No, it's all okay. I promise. If you're going to be seen with me, then you need to look good."

"I wouldn't expect anything less."

The bartender returned and placed the beer in front of Jules.

"Let that settle a bit, miss, before you drink."

"Sure…thanks."

Jules looked up at the television.

"Not much else with the news," Joe said. "Still counting the dead and dying. They're still talking about the difference in the United States."

"If only they knew the whole story."

Joe stared at Jules.

"It's just surreal," Jules continued, "knowing what we know and then watching things unfold in front of us like this. It doesn't seem real, you know?"

"I agree." Joe leaned forward towards Jules and spoke quietly. "The bartender is pretty pissed at the idea that the US knew something but did nothing to help everyone else."

"Yeah, well, what would he think if he knew the whole story?"

"I don't know. Why don't you ask?"

"Yeah...right." She rolled her eyes.

Joe leaned over to look in the bags on the other side of his chair. Inside, he saw two pairs of denim jeans, a blue sweatshirt, and a button-down flannel shirt in tartan plaid. When he looked back up, Jules was gone. He turned around and looked back towards the bar where she was already talking to the bartender. He stood up quickly.

"...really, miss, I think they've forgotten us. We go to war, but they let us die now. It's not right."

"You mean the vaccine?" Jules asked.

"Yeah, it's not right. They should've given us a chance. They knew and did nothing. It's bloody nuts."

"What are they saying about the vaccine development on the TV?" Jules asked.

"They don't know. Some secret program. I don't buy it."

"Why not?"

"No way it was secret. You can't keep something like that a secret. They all knew."

"We just came from the US. I can tell you...nobody knew."

"Right... Sure."

"What if I told you that they killed some people on purpose to develop the vaccine? Would that change your opinion?"

"I don't know."

"Would it make a difference if they killed a few people to save more?" Her voice grew louder. "What if the people they killed didn't get a chance to say no? What if other people were killed because they tried to stop the development of the vaccine?"

Joe put his arm around Jules and tried to turn her away from the bar, but she shrugged his arm off her shoulder.

"...you don't see the whole picture, sir. All you're seeing is that the Americans seemed to have saved some lives."

"A bunch of lives, miss."

"Does that make a difference?"

The two men at the corner table listened as Jules spoke more loudly.

The bartender leaned forward and pointed as he spoke. "Well, I think it does. It's easy for you to talk when your people are the ones still alive. It's our people who are dying."

"We need to leave," Joe said and pulled Jules away from the bar. "This is not the place to discuss this."

They walked back to the table and gathered their sacks, but Jules's gaze remained fixed on the bartender. Joe put his arm around her and led her towards the door.

"None of you understand. Not really," Jules shouted over her shoulder as Joe pushed her through the door out onto the sidewalk.

"That's enough!" Joe kept her moving forward. "You can't do that sort of thing here."

"I know…but I can't stand for people to judge so easily."

"We can't help that. We just can't. We can't change their opinions. The true story will get out, but until that happens, we have to keep quiet."

"I know, Joe. I'm sorry, but…" Jules remained silent.

They walked towards the parked car to leave the city and drive back to the north. Neither spoke any more of the events. The bustle of people had diminished across Princes Street in Edinburgh. Sunlight dimmed some, but darkness was distant in the summer night of the far north latitude. Complete darkness was brief, restricted to the confines of midnight to four a.m. Winter was the opposite, with dark prevailing for more than fourteen hours a day. The days would shorten, they knew, with night overtaking day.

They stayed in Scotland through the season, until days once again became longer than nights.

- author's postscript -

Recognizing the complex military environment after World War II, the United States government maintained active weapons research and development across multiple armament types: conventional, nuclear, chemical, and biological. The development included both offensive and defensive capabilities, but the line between offense and defense blurred at times.

The chemical and biological weapons programs peaked in intensity in the late 1950s and early 1960s, with the research and testing spread across multiple sites in the United States. The largest programs were located at, but not limited to, Fort Detrick in Maryland, the Dugway Proving Grounds in Utah, and the Pine Bluff Arsenal in Arkansas.

In 1969, at the urging of National Security Advisor Henry Kissinger, President Nixon unilaterally discontinued the United States' research and development in biological and most chemical weapons. Hailed at the time as a forward-thinking step, the Presidential declaration led to a worldwide ban in 1972, with the signing of the Biological Weapons Convention in Geneva. However, without significant research into new weapons, the United States' ability to conduct defensive biological weapons research was also severely restricted.

Given the rudimentary state of biotechnology in the early 1970s, advanced engineering of biological weapons was restricted to weapon delivery, not the weapon itself. With the advent of recombinant DNA technology in the late 1970's and 1980's, engineered bacteria and viruses became a reality. In violation of the Biological Weapons Convention of 1972, many countries, including the USSR, maintained active biological weapons programs, including work towards engineering the microbes to improve environmental stability, lower infectious dose, and increase antibiotic resistance.

Intelligence limitations of the CIA and political limitations inside the United States left the door open for clandestine development of weapons programs elsewhere. The Soviet Program, known as the Biopreparat, remained active both offensively and defensively, employing at its peak over fifty thousand people. Its capacity for weapons production was measured not in tons but in hundreds of tons for each of at least nine separate agents, including those causing plague, tularemia, anthrax, smallpox, and Venezuelan equine encephalomyelitis. The program, only a rumor in the CIA, continued its work unabated for over fifteen years, even in the face of a horrific accident in 1979 at Sverdlovsk that likely killed over one thousand people. The Soviets denied the incident was related to a secret biological weapons program for thirteen years, until President Boris Yeltsin admitted the existence of the program in 1992.

The threat that biological weapons pose is perhaps greater today than it has ever been in the past. The present environment is more complex with rogue governments and well-financed and organized terrorist organizations. Modern biotechnology, now relatively inexpensive and readily available, may prove to be especially deadly in the new world of biological weapons. With the failure of intelligence in respect to the massive Soviet program in the past, there is little hope that the same present day intelligence-gathering entities will ever successfully infiltrate much smaller and more motivated terrorist organizations to stop a new threat. This new threat of biological attack on the United States will force incredibly difficult decisions on the leaders of the defensive response.

Acknowledgements

Writing a book has been a daunting task for me. It is certainly not something done in a vacuum. I am indebted to many people without whom this work would have never been completed.

First and foremost is my family who have endured in the past and present (and I'm sure in the future) my many oddities. Tolerance is what makes a family function.

Many people contributed comments along the way in reading various forms of this manuscript. P. Bean, S. Bean, C. Hardin, K. Prince (and family), P. Oden, and N. Blochberger were all 'first readers.' I do pity the pain of reading a rough draft, but appreciate more than you know the encouragement for me to keep trying.

I am also indebted to 'late' readers of this work. M. Carlton, B. Brooks, K. Kuhn, and C. Holdsworth were all wonderfully critical. A true friend is one who will tell you when your nose is not clean.

Others read, and tolerated, the manuscript and to those I have not mentioned, it is not my intention to slight your efforts on my behalf, but in the interest of brevity I cannot list everyone. My appreciation abounds.

To the readers in the future, I hope you will continue to support me and others who choose to put pen to paper, and please support your local small bookstore. Independence is a gift that is both rare and valuable.